Readers love the Cowboy Nobility series
by ANDREW GREY

The Duke's Cowboy

"If you are not yet a fan of Andrew Grey who writes stories of love and who always manages to get my emotions working overtime, then you are missing out on some amazing reading."

—Paranormal Romance Guild

"Both men have issues that need to be addressed before they can commit to each other—and they do. This is a romance after all so there's a HEA that satisfies."

—Sparkling Book Reviews

The Viscount's Rancher

"Andrew Grey fans will be very happy how it turns out, and romance fans in general will be as well."

—Love Bytes

Published by DREAMSPINNER PRESS
www.dreamspinnerpress.com

By Andrew Grey (cont)

FOREVER YOURS
Can't Live Without You
Never Let You Go

GOOD FIGHT
The Good Fight • The Fight Within
The Fight for Identity
Takoda and Horse

HEARTS ENTWINED
Heart Unseen • Heart Unheard
Heart Untouched • Heart Unbroken

HEARTWARD
Heartward • Homeward

HOLIDAY STORIES
Copping a Sweetest Day Feel
Cruise for Christmas
Frosty the Schnauzer
A Lion in Tails
Mariah the Christmas Moose
A Present in Swaddling Clothes
Rudolph the Rescue Jack Russell
Secret Guncle • Simple Gifts
Snowbound in Nowhere
Stardust • Sweet Anticipation
With Amy Lane: Holiday Cheer
Anthology

LAS VEGAS ESCORTS
The Price • The Gift

LOVE MEANS…
Love Means… No Shame
Love Means… Courage
Love Means… No Boundaries
Love Means… Freedom
Love Means … No Fear
Love Means… Healing
Love Means… Family
Love Means… Renewal
Love Means… No Limits
Love Means… Patience
Love Means… Endurance

LOVE'S CHARTER
Setting the Hook • Ebb and Flow

MUST LOVE DOGS
Rescue Me • Rescue Us
Rudolph the Rescue Jack Russell
Secret Guncle • Frosty the Schnauzer

NEW LEAF ROMANCES
New Leaf • In the Weeds

PAINT BY NUMBER
Paint By Number
The Northern Lights in His Eyes

Published by DREAMSPINNER PRESS
www.dreamspinnerpress.com

Published by DREAMSPINNER PRESS
www.dreamspinnerpress.com

The Earl's Wrangler

ANDREW GREY

Published by
DREAMSPINNER PRESS

8219 Woodville Hwy #1245
Woodville, FL 32362 USA
www.dreamspinnerpress.com

The Earl's Wrangler
© 2025 Andrew Grey

Cover Art
© 2025 L.C. Chase
http://www.lcchase.com
Cover content is for illustrative purposes only and any person depicted on the cover is a model.

Trade Paperback ISBN: 9781641088312
Digital ISBN: 9781641088305
Trade Paperback published September 2025
v. 1.0

CHAPTER 1

"I TAKE it you're back in England," Randall Whealton, Earl of Plymouth, said as he settled into his favorite leather chair at the club in London. "I don't understand how you can spend so much time out in the wilds."

He didn't come to the club as often as he would have liked. His father had been a member, as had his grandfather before him. It was something members of his family did, and Randall actually liked it. Yes, the place was stodgy and slow to change, but in a way it felt like home. There was something comforting about the company of other men, friends he and his family had developed over generations.

"Yes. Well…." George slowly lowered himself into one of the chairs across from him, his partner sitting next to him. Randall couldn't help noticing both men. They were handsome, and Alan particularly so, with his sun-kissed skin and the most intense eyes Randall had ever seen. He and George had known each other since they were ten, and he considered George, now Duke of Northumberland, a relatively close friend. Alan, on the other hand, was a completely unknown quantity as far as Randall was concerned, and therefore someone to be skeptical of. "Alan and I arrived in England last week. We were back in Wyoming for a month to help Alan's family. There's a lot to be done this time of year, and it really is beautiful there."

Randall shuddered but did his level best not to show it. He could think of nothing worse than spending an entire month away from the civility of England. "I suppose everywhere has its charms if you look hard enough for them."

Alan cleared his throat. George gently tapped his hand, and Alan nodded but sat a little taller before turning the full impact of his gaze on Randall. "Now just how far up your ass have you pushed that stick?" There was no heat in his comment, and Randall figured Alan meant it as a joke, but he tightened his hold on his glass and blinked a few times before letting the remark pass. He was not about to make a scene or draw attention, not here.

George snickered, but Randall refused to rise to anyone's bait. "I'm just saying that I like it here. It's civil, with all the comforts of home."

"Ones you don't need to work for," Alan added. He had a reputation for speaking plainly, and Randall had met him before and knew how Alan was. But his holier-than-thou attitude got under his skin. The truth was that he didn't really like the man, but was well-mannered enough not to let it show, especially since he was George's partner. And yet he was a little jealous of how Alan felt comfortable enough to say what was on his mind without all the social beating around the bush.

One of the attendants approached, bringing him a refill of his Cognac, and Randall lifted the large glass, inhaling the deep, rich scent of the spirit before taking a sip from his glass. The attendant offered one to Goerge and Alan.

"Thank you," George said.

"Can I have a whiskey, neat?" Alan said with a smile. "Thank you very much. I appreciate it." And damned if the attendant didn't smile back at him. These men were trained to be attentive and as unobtrusive as possible.

Randall cleared his throat, and the attendant's smile disappeared in an instant.

"Don't be a dick to the guy. I like him. The last time George dragged me to this place, he was helpful and kept me from making a fool of myself," Alan told him as he shook his head, the attendant already on his errand to get the ordered refreshments.

Too late for that, Randall thought to himself. This was a place for gentlemen, and Randall knew what that meant. Alan sat back, those long legs stretching out as he made himself comfortable. Maybe that was part of why Alan got under his skin. The man always seemed so damned comfortable wherever he went. He was sitting in Randall's own club, and yet he looked as though he owned the place. Other members came up and unobtrusively greeted Alan, shaking his hand and speaking quietly before moving on. Others nodded and shared a quick smile before moving into the club room. The man seemed so damned at ease with everyone and everything.

Even Montague, Marquess of Lowrey, one of the oldest and most decorous members in the establishment, seemed happy to see Alan. "How are your horses this year, Harlan?" Alan asked as he passed by, practically shouting by club standards. On top of that, he referred to one of the senior peers in the country by his first name, and the marquess didn't even bat an eye. Something was quite wrong, especially for a man like the marquess, who always prided himself on tradition and, well, normalcy.

"Alan, my boy," he said. "They are doing wonderfully. Your help was greatly appreciated. You and George should come and see them now." The man was practically giddy and actually patted Alan on the shoulder.

"I look forward to it," Alan said, not politely but with genuine interest. "And if your team needs anything, let me know." Alan was smiling at one of the oldest and most notorious grumps in England and getting a smile in return. "Over here I sometimes feel like a duck out of water, but with horses, I know I'm at home."

Harlan met Randall's gaze and nodded, his face falling back to his usual dour expression, and then he left the room. The attendant returned and set the drinks on the table before silently turning away.

"Thanks, Jimmy," Alan said and sipped the whiskey. Then he stood. "I'll be back."

Randall wondered where he was going, but it was none of his business.

"Have fun. The billiard room is down to the right," George added, and Alan turned, picked up his glass, and headed out. Both Randall and George followed him with their eyes, but judging by the heat in George's, it was for very different reasons.

Randall shook his head as he watched Alan go. "Is he always like that? It must get exhausting."

George smiled. "Yes. He's honest and forthright. You always know where you stand with him. There's no subterfuge or polite obfuscation. If he's unhappy or angry, there's no doubt about it." He sighed softly. "And everyone seems to love him for it. I know I do."

Randall and George had been interested in each other at one time, but that was years ago, and nothing had come of it. "Including Harlan, apparently," Randall commented.

George leaned forward in the chair, sipping from his snifter after swirling the amber liquid. "I took him to the races last year, and one of Harlan's horses was running. It did moderately well, but when I introduced him to Harlan after the race, Alan told him everything he thought was wrong. Harlan looked about ready to bite his head off, but Alan just smiled and said, 'Don't worry, we can fix it if you like.' Then he went on to make suggestions, and you saw the result this time around. Alan can seem abrupt, but he's genuine."

Randall took another sip and set his glass on the table. "I'm too damned English to be that genuine."

George laughed outright, and others in the room turned. He quieted instantly, his own English reserve returning. "Sometimes I think I am too, but Alan is a breath of fresh air, and it's really difficult not to inhale deeply." He settled back in the chair now that Alan had disappeared from view.

Things grew quiet between them as George enjoyed his drink and Randall mulled over the questions that raced through his mind. "He called the marquess Harlan… and got away with it."

George chuckled. "He doesn't get the peerage thing at all. Titles mean nothing to him."

"Using them is a sign of respect," Randall said. He often hid behind the veneer of his title, especially when he was feeling particularly uncomfortable.

"The only time Alan uses my title is when he's angry with me. It took me a long time to begin to understand him. When I first brought him to the estate, I wondered if he would fit in. Instead, he learned who every person was who worked there and treated them all the same way. He worked harder than anyone—still does. But I will say this: if Alan gives you respect, it isn't because of position or rank—it's because you earned it." George finished the last of his drink and set the glass aside. "Thank you for the drink. I understand there's to be cards in about an hour. Are you going to play?"

Randall nodded. "You know me. I'm always up for cards." It was one of the things he was truly good at. When playing, he had a very good read on the other players and almost always came out ahead.

"Excellent. I'm going to check on Alan, but I'll see you in an hour." George flashed him a genuine smile before leaving the room. Randall watched him go, wondering why Alan unleveled his world so easily and why the room felt a little duller now that he and George had left.

THE CARD room was fairly full when Randall entered. The club staff was ready with chips and had the tables set up the same way they had been for decades. Most regular players had seats they preferred, and Randall headed for his only to find Alan sitting in it. Of course. He swallowed and took a chair at the same table, sitting next to the marquess and across from George.

"Now, my cowboy friend, no cleaning me out the way you did last time," the marquess said seriously. Cards were always serious business in the club.

"I'll take it easy on you. I don't want Madeline angry with me," Alan replied with that huge smile of his, while others sat down, filling the spaces at the table. The card stewards made their rounds so everyone could buy in. This was a gentleman's club, so no money actually changed hands at the tables. All money was handled through the club in a discreet manner. Alan, since he was a guest, must have made prior arrangements, because the stewards simply gave him what he requested.

They cut the cards to see who would deal first, and Randall gathered the cards and dealt the first hand.

Everyone seemed to be feeling each other out, so there were no large moves at first, but after a few hands, things became more spirited. Randall won two small pots, enough to put him slightly ahead, which was good, but games of cards lasted for hours, and more than anything, he wanted to wipe the smile off that damned cowboy's face.

"I'M FINISHED for today," the marquess said as he tossed in his hand. "I've lost enough to you," he told Alan, who had the largest stack of chips at the table. "Madeline will be upset if I continue." He patted Alan on the shoulder.

"You tell that lovely wife of yours that I said hello and that the next time you visit I should have that old carriage you found at your place ready for the two of you to take a ride."

"She is going to love that," the marquess said before nodding to the others at the table and leaving the room, using his cane for support.

Throughout the evening, the number of tables had diminished and the players had condensed down to fewer tables until only their table was left. "I think this is my last hand," Alan said as he turned to George.

"You need to give us a chance to get even," Randall said, looking down at his comparatively meager stack of chips.

"What I need to do is stop before you lose any more," Alan said gently, but Randall's temper rose, and he had to remind himself to stay calm and not give anything away. "George, it's your deal," Alan said as he tossed in his initial chips. Randall did the same as the others at the table slid their chairs back.

"I'm out."

"So am I," the other players said.

"It looks like it's just us." No one else to get in the way. Randall had been studying Alan all evening, and he was pretty sure he'd gotten a sense of when Alan was bluffing. George dealt the cards and let the two of them play.

Randall was dealt a possible outside straight with a paired eight. Alan bet, and Randall raised him two hundred pounds, which drew the attention of the others still observing. "You're going to have to pay to play."

"Call," Alan said coolly, and they each took one card, which Randall thought interesting. He'd broken his pair of eights, and lo and behold, he hit the straight. When Alan bet, Randall raised once more, this time five hundred pounds.

Alan sat calmly and raised as well, this time a thousand pounds. "I don't have enough here to cover that," Randall said, knowing the club rules were always table stakes. It helped head off any number of issues between the members, especially where money was concerned.

Alan set his cards facedown. "Care for a little side wager? If you win, I'll pay out as if you called."

"And if you win?" Randall asked.

Alan glanced at George. "Then you work off the debt."

"At George's estate? What's the point?" Randall shrugged.

"No, at my family ranch. George will be returning for a couple of weeks in October, and if I win, then you work off the debt in Wyoming, to my mother's satisfaction." There was a sparkle in those damned blue eyes.

"All right. I call you." There was no need to push his chips in the middle, so he sat back and then showed his cards. "A straight, nine to the king." He was fairly sure he had the winning hand. Alan had blinked more than once when he'd gotten his last card, which, according to his past play, meant he hadn't gotten the card he'd wanted.

"Looks like you're going to be mucking out stalls," Alan said as he showed a full house. "Jacks full of eights." He sat back, and Randall gaped for a second before standing and reaching across the table. This was a gentleman's game, and win or lose, he had no intention of showing just how angry and upset he was with himself. He had let Alan bait him, and now in his haste to put Alan in his place, his mouth had written a check that the rest of him would have to cash. Alan took his hand, and they shook before Randall pulled his hand back and stood.

The game steward approached Alan, presumably regarding payment. "What arrangements would you like made?"

Alan picked up two of the hundred-pound chips and handed them to the steward. "Make sure everyone who served us gets a share. And make sure Harlan is made whole. I don't want him to get in trouble with his wife. She hates it when he plays cards." He winked, and damned if the steward didn't nod.

"Of course."

"The rest put on George's account." Alan drank the last of the whiskey in his glass. "We'll be in touch to let you know about the trip to Wyoming. Who knows—you might find out you like it."

"Alan…," George said. "Randall, you really don't need to go. He isn't going to hold you to that. Alan is just teasing you."

Alan nodded. "You can donate the shortfall to a worthy charity."

Randall cleared his throat. "No. A wager is a point of honor." There was no way in hell he was going to owe Alan anything. Yes, he might be offering to let him off the hook, but Randall knew that if he agreed, then every time Alan told this story, he'd be able to gloat at how Randall had taken the easy way out. That was something he could not live with. Alan and the Duke might be married, but that didn't mean that Randall was going to be in any way indebted to a hick cowboy from Wyoming.

He had many faults, but his father had drummed into his head that a man always honored his debts and that not doing so endangered not only his honor, but that of the family as well. It was one of the few lessons his father had ever bothered to try to teach him. He and his father did not see eye to eye on much. Randall was fairly sure that if the old man could have disinherited him for being gay, he would have. But he was now the oldest and the only boy, so the title and all land and property associated with it went to him because primogeniture was the law of the land, even today.

"Then we'll send you all the information you need to know just as soon as we make the arrangements," Alan said.

Randall nodded, meeting his gaze, because he refused to back down. George then guided Alan out toward the cloak room.

Randall sank into a chair and ordered a double Scotch, neat, from a passing server and downed it as soon as it was brought. He hated making a fool of himself, and he could certainly grit his teeth and manage living on a ranch for two weeks, all the way out in the middle of nowhere, away from the comforts he'd very much grown accustomed to. But damn it all, one way or another, he'd figure out a way through this.

CHAPTER 2

THE SOUND of horses approaching roused Sawyer Kinkaid in the early morning, and he climbed out of his bedroll, standing and stretching as a pair of riders approached where he'd spent the night in the back of his old truck. He groaned as the oldest of the Justice boys came into view. He had met Alan just the one time, when he was hired three months ago. Right after that, Alan had returned to England, and Sawyer had begun settling into his life here. "Have you been out here all night?"

"Yes. I had work to do, and it was easier to stay so I could start again first thing and make sure the herd didn't find the weak spot." He scratched his side. "Mrs. Justice understood."

"Of course," Alan said as he slipped down off his horse. The man was every bit the cowboy from head to toe. "This is George."

"It's a pleasure," the other man said, and instantly Sawyer knew who he was. He'd heard stories about Alan and his husband, the duke.

"Thank you, your dukeness." He wondered if he was required to bow or something, but figured to hell with it. Who the fuck was going to care—the steers and cows a hundred yards off?

"Just call me George. Out here I don't use my title." He turned to Alan, and almost instantly, Sawyer felt a stab of regret almost as hard as a poke in the side from a knife. The way Alan and George looked at each other made his insides twist and ache in a way he thought he had well under control. There had been someone who gazed at him like that once— at least he had thought so—but in the end, Sawyer had been wrong, just like he was most of the time when it came to people. Not that the loss hurt any less, even though it probably had been his own fault. He was as bad at reading people as he was skilled with horses and cattle.

Sawyer turned away, unable to stand the sight of the love that shone between them. "What can I do for you?" he asked. "I have this section of fence that needs to be mended. I found it last night, and the repair was going to take longer than I had light for, so I stayed here to keep the beasties away."

"Mother hadn't heard from you, and she was a little worried," Alan explained. Sawyer felt bad for making Mrs. Justice concerned. She had enough to do without wondering about him.

George snorted. "Please. Don't lie to the man. She mentioned that you were out here, and since we just arrived, he was looking for an excuse to go for a ride. Maureen said that she had messaged you and you didn't respond."

Sawyer pulled out his phone and tapped the screen, but it remained dark. Crap, he must have forgotten to plug it in before he left. "Tell her I'm fine, please. I'll charge my phone when I get back to the barn later." A white device sailed through the air, and he caught it out of instinct.

"Use that to charge it. That way you won't be alone out here if something happens."

Sawyer plugged in his phone and set it and the battery thing in the bed of the truck, not telling them that being out here alone and on his own was how he liked it. When he was away from everyone, he didn't have to worry that he didn't understand their jokes or the looks that people gave one another, or that he was the butt of whatever story was being told and had no idea.

"Thank you," he said, just because he knew it was the right response. "I need to get this finished, and then I want to check the rest of this run." He looked north toward the mountains. "I promise to keep my phone on in case someone needs me." Maybe that would get them to leave him alone so he could go back to work.

George climbed down off his horse and opened one of his saddlebags. He pulled out a satchel and handed it to him. "Maureen sent you some coffee and breakfast. And she put in some sandwiches because she figured you'd probably stay out all day."

Now Sawyer smiled. No one made coffee like Mrs. J. "I'll thank her for the provisions." He opened the thermos, inhaled, and then drank right out of it, the hot, smooth liquid sliding down his throat.

"See that you do," Alan said and then winked at him. Sawyer hoped that meant the stern expression wasn't actually real, though he wondered for a second.

"He's kidding you. We'll see you back at the house when you're done." George mounted his horse once more, and Alan did the same. Then the two of them rode away to the northeast, leaving Sawyer alone, which was perfect as far as he was concerned.

Sawyer opened the tube of foil and ate the two warm egg-and-ham biscuits inside. They tasted like heaven. That was one of the wonderful things about the Justice ranch. The food was always really good, and Mrs. J treated all the people who worked for her like they were family. That was probably why it was so difficult to get a job here—folks rarely left. It wasn't like other places that seemed to have revolving doors on the bunkhouse. What was even more amazing was that the place was actually three ranches, or it had been at one time. Mrs. J had apparently kept her own name to avoid confusion after she married Claude. Together they managed their land as well as that of a third ranch that they leased. At least that was what Sawyer had been told. It wasn't any of his business. He was just grateful for the job at a good place with good people who were willing to let him do what he did best. He drank some more coffee and then set the rest of the food in the cab of the truck out of the sun and got back to work.

After cutting away the broken lines of fencing, he found himself looking out the way Alan and George had gone. He couldn't see them any longer, which probably meant they had entered the line of trees around the creek that flowed in that direction. They might have the time for fun, but Sawyer was being paid to get his work done. He went back to stringing the fence lines, doing a good enough job that he wouldn't need to return to this area for a while. Once he was done, he checked over his work and loaded the tools and supplies into the back of the truck. He also took the opportunity to check his phone and send Mrs. J a message thanking her for the breakfast and coffee. Then he climbed in and drove off down the two-track access road, checking over the rest of the fence line.

"WERE YOU intending to stay out all week?" Chip asked with a grin as he met Sawyer in the yard once his truck pulled to a stop. He was Mrs. J's second son and one of the most open and easy-to-read people Sawyer knew. They had become friends of a sort. "I thought I was going to miss you entirely."

"Just overnight," Sawyer told him. "How long are you here?"

Chip was in college to be a veterinarian. At least that was what he was training for. Everyone said his plans were to come back and take over the ranch, as well as open a practice on the property. Eventually his mama and Claude would retire to travel, and Chip would run the entire place.

"Just a week. I had my midterms, and then they gave us a break before we finish the semester. They don't usually, but there's some big gathering of the professors going on, so they adjusted the term."

"I met your brother and his…." Sawyer never knew the right term to use, so he let his voice trail off.

"Husband. Alan and George got married a few years ago." He turned toward the house. "They said they were going out for a ride." He snickered softly.

"They stopped by where I was working before heading on north." He pulled down the tailgate and began unloading the fence supplies. Chip grabbed a wheel of wire, and they walked to the supply barn together.

"Yeah. That's their favorite spot. They always go out there, and when they come back, they have these huge, dopey smiles." Chip set the wire where it belonged, and Sawyer put the extra posts with the others. He sighed. "They brought a friend with them from England. The last time they did that, it was Collin, and he was really cool. But I'm not so sure about this guy."

They returned to the truck for the last of the tools and supplies before Sawyer pushed the tailgate back into place. "Okay." He had never met this Collin and Tank, though he knew the Justice ranch now included what had once been Tank's place. It was a little confusing to him, but he tried to keep it all straight. "Why not?"

"You met George, right? He's a duke and a really good guy. Got more money than God, but not snooty or nothing. And Collin was really cool. He's a viscount and has an estate in England that he and Tank are running. When he was here, he mucked stalls and helped with the steers and everything. I'm the godfather to their son, Archie. They just adopted him a few months ago." He leaned against the truck. "This guy they brought is an earl or something, and he's…." Chip shrugged in that happy way he had. "I don't know. Maybe the guy is just grumpy because of jet lag. Ain't sure. But when Mama offered him coffee, he asked for tea, and not just any tea, but lightly steeped Darjeeling with just a hint of milk." He shook his head. "What the fuck is that? Ain't nobody drinking tea on a ranch."

"Don't much care what a man drinks," Sawyer said flatly. Chip liked to talk, and Sawyer was fine with listening. He never passed on what he heard, and sometimes Chip just needed someone to tell stuff to.

"I suppose not," Chip agreed, deflating slightly.

"Where is he now?"

"Last I saw he was still in bed. But it's only nine in the morning, and the guy is really green. Like I swear he ain't done a real day's work in his life."

"Not likely to even if he's here."

Chip got excited again. "That's the funny thing. Alan said that this earl guy lost a bet and that he has to work it off here. It was part of the bet or something."

"Well, we'll see how that goes." Sawyer moved away from the truck. "I got work to do or your mama will be asking about stuff, and I don't want to disappoint her. And I'm sure that you have things you need to do. A week off school don't mean you don't have homework or anything."

Chip waved him off. "I can do that later."

"No. You get it done. I never got the chance to go to college. All I know is ranching, and I'll be shoveling shit and breaking horses until my knees give out and I can't move anymore. That work is more important than whatever you were thinkin' of doing. Your mama says you're gonna be a vet. So be the best one you can be."

Chip stepped back, grinning, and gave him a salute. "Aye, aye, captain." He turned and hurried into the house.

Sawyer pulled open the truck door, got out the sandwiches from earlier, and ate them quickly. It had been hours of work since he'd last eaten, and he was hungry. Once he was done, he headed to the barn, let the remaining horses out into their paddocks, and started cleaning up the stalls. Like he'd told Chip, there was always a lot to do.

"RANDALL," SAWYER heard Alan say as he was finishing up the work in the barn, "we got plenty of work lined up for you."

"I just got up," the guy with him groaned.

"This is a ranch," Alan said as they drew closer. Sawyer put his tools away and grabbed a broom to sweep the aisle. He liked his barn to be as clean as possible. It kept the place smelling fresh, and he was convinced it kept the horses healthier. He hated flies buzzing around. "It's nearly noon, and everyone here has already been working for six hours."

"No way."

Three pair of boots appeared in front of him, and before Sawyer could stop himself, he swept dirt and bits of manure all over them.

"Watch what you're doing," the stranger snapped. "Look what you did."

Sawyer blinked, surprised for just a moment. "This is a barn, and I'm working. You need to watch where you're going." He paused in his work, straightened his back, and stood toe to toe with the stranger. Then he stepped back. Alan and George moved out of the way, and Sawyer swept the rest of the pile all over the now even dirtier boots. Then he turned away and continued with his task.

"You saw that?" the guy who had to be the Earl of Assholes said. "He can't do that."

"Sure he can, Randall," George told him.

"You were in the way, and just so you know, your earlness isn't going to get any special treatment here. You want people to respect you, then earn it. And if you get in the way of the work, you get mucked boots. Get in the way of a horse and you'll get hit. If you get in the way of the cattle, you could be trampled. Nothing gets out of the way for you." Alan seemed to be laying down the law. "Now, you're here for two weeks, and you're going to work in the barn with Sawyer here."

"Excuse me?" Randall said.

"Yeah. Sawyer is one of our best hands, and you're always saying you know horses. Well, one thing is for sure—at the end of two weeks, you're going to know how to clean up their crap."

Sawyer swallowed hard. "Are you sure that's a good idea? Your mama said that she has three colts that she got at auction coming in. She asked me to get them settled and to start training them up. It's going to take a lot of my time and…."

Alan smiled. "That's perfect. You'll need some help, and Randall here can give you that. He can clean the stalls and anything else while you work with the colts." If Sawyer didn't know any better, he'd think Alan was having a good time with this. Sawyer had figured that Randall was a friend of his and that he was having him on with this whole bet thing, but maybe there was more to it than that. "You up to that?" he asked Randall.

"Sure, I can help in here." Randall looked about as thrilled as if he had been asked to help out in a slaughterhouse.

"Great. Sawyer here can explain what needs to be done." Alan and George left the barn, leaving the two of them alone.

"There's always things to be done. You can clean the tack." Sawyer motioned to the back, and Randall headed that way. Sawyer followed and did his best not to watch the attractive backside in the fancy jeans. "You might want to get boots and clothes made for working. Those fancy duds are going to get really dirty, and they ain't going to hold up."

"I'll ask George about it," he said, as though Sawyer wasn't good enough. It didn't matter if a man looked like he walked out of a magazine, with dark blond wavy hair down to his shoulders that looked like a mane. He swallowed and shook his head. Sawyer needed to wipe out any thoughts of how good Randall looked or—when he passed him to go into the tack room—how the man smelled, like summer rain. Fucking hell, he was not going to do this.

"All the tack needs to be cleaned. Everything is in here." He opened the cupboard. "I'm sure your earlness knows what to do." He didn't wait for him to answer before leaving to return to work.

CHAPTER 3

RANDALL SHOOK his head and sighed as he worked the leather bridle with his fingers. It was old and in desperate need of some care. He'd worked on a number of other pieces and had set them aside. One thing he could say: the room was meticulously organized, with every horse's gear clearly labeled. It was plain that for the most part, everything had been well cared for, even if some of the tack needed more than cleaning.

Sawyer hadn't been back, but Randall heard him moving around outside. Occasionally wood slid along concrete, and Randall wondered if the man was building something or tearing it down. Not that it was any of his business. He was here because he'd been stupid and lost a bet. If it was Alan's goal to show him how great Wyoming was, it wasn't working. All Randall wanted was to return to England and his home, where he'd spend weeks washing the crud off, enjoying proper tea, and spending his afternoons on the estate, playing lord of the manor to the hordes of tourists who visited the home built by the second earl during the Restoration. He was damned proud of it and the work his grandfather, father, and he had done to restore and preserve it.

The dragging came again, the sound grating up his back. Randall finished the bridle and put it back where he'd found it before poking his head out of the room. "What in bloody hell are you doing?"

Sawyer continued dragging the old piece of furniture out of what had once been a stall. "What does it look like?" he snapped. "There are three colts coming in. I only got two stalls, so I need to clean out the one that everyone has filled with shit over the last decade." He continued dragging the old kitchen sideboard out of the stall. "I was thinking I'd toss this on the burn pile out back." He continued dragging, and Randall waved his hand.

"No." He drew closer as Sawyer stared at him like he was crazy. He licked his finger and brushed it over the dry wood. "This has seen a hard life, but it's not junk." He needed more time and better light to really see, but even without getting into the detail, he knew this was not something to be broken up and burned. "Is there a storage place, somewhere dry?"

"There's the workshop," Sawyer offered.

"Then let's take it there. I'll help you." He looked it over and lifted at the top, which separated from the base. "It's in pieces."

"If you say so. This is just junk. It's been in here forever." Sawyer took the other side, his arms bulging as he lifted. Randall let him lead the way, and they carried the sections out of the barn and into the work shed, then put them back together along the one wall. Sawyer stepped back, looking at it. "I still say it's not worth any time."

"We'll see," Randall told him.

Sawyer shrugged and left the shed. "There's plenty of work to do."

Randall's stomach rumbled. "When do you eat?" He realized it had been hours.

"It's only four in the afternoon. We'll have dinner when it starts getting dark. Once the work is finished." He strode back into the barn, and Randall wanted to throttle him, but he still couldn't help admiring the way he filled out those damned tight jeans.

"I see you're helping Sawyer," George said as he approached, handing Randall a mug. "I thought you might need something."

"The man is a pain in the ass," Randall said, then hummed at the lovely tea. "Reminds me of home." He closed his eyes, letting the smooth, warm liquid slide down his throat.

George chuckled. "Yeah, but you keep watching him."

Randall rolled his eyes. "The wrapping may be pleasant, but the inside is filled with asshole. No thank you."

"It isn't like you've been at your most pleasant." George swept his arms around him. "Look at this place. The mountains are so beautiful, and just breathe. The air is fresh and clean. Every morning, I step outside and see this and I'm just happy." A pack of dogs hurried over, all of them settling around George, who petted and spoke to each of them. "How can you be so sour?"

"I was the one who was happy to stay at home."

George lifted his gaze upward to the clear blue sky. "You're here, so make the most of it. This is a totally new experience for you. Let yourself enjoy it, rather than being a Debbie Downer." He grinned.

"Those American sayings…," Randall said flatly.

"I know. Don't you love them?" He sipped the last of his tea. "These people say what they mean. If they like you, they will move heaven and earth for you. They live off the land, and it's a hard life, but they're strong people." George leaned closer. "And I can tell you that strength is sexy as all fuck. Look at Alan." Goerge grinned. "Heck, bloody look at Sawyer," he said just as Sawyer came out of the barn with a barrow full of junk. It had to be heavy, judging by the way his muscles flexed. "See what I mean?" He nudged Randall, who shook his head. There was no way in hell he was going to get involved with anyone. He was here for two weeks, and that was bloody well it.

"Doesn't matter," Randall said with emphasis that he knew was too quick and forceful. "I'm staying a couple of weeks and then I'm going home, never to return." George snickered like a kid. "And don't bring up Haferton. He came over here because he was tired of England and wanted to meet someone like Alan. I personally don't see the attraction."

"Then you aren't looking in the right direction, my friend. Most of these men are the strong, silent type. They know who they are, and when they see something they want, they go after it." George turned to watch him, and Randall could almost feel the intensity in his gaze. "Most of the time. You see Dusty over there? That man rides bulls. Every year he represents this ranch in the local rodeo. He wins too. And Kevin over there? His specialty is cattle roping. He can tie up a calf faster than you can say 'holy shit.' Okay? They have no fear… until it comes to the people they like. Dusty is currently dating a girl in town, but it took him six months to get up the courage to ask her out."

"Why? Dusty is a good-looking man," Randall said. "I'm surprised he isn't beating them off with a stick."

"Well, it's part of that silent thing that these guys have going on. They can do shit that would break their necks and love every second of it. But when it comes to the heart…." George shrugged.

"What is it you're trying to say?"

"That you're just like these guys, only louder. You talk all the goddamn time, but you're just as stunted as the rest of them. I'm not saying that you should jump Sawyer's bones, but stop being a dick and you might find out that these men could end up being the best friends you've ever had in your life."

"George!"

"Who is that?" Randall asked.

"Chip, Alan's brother." George waved, and Chip hurried over.

"I need your help. Got a calf that needs pulling, and I could use some help keeping Mama calm. This one is a nervous Nellie." George handed Randall the mug, and Chip practically pulled him away. Randall set the mugs on the back stoop before returning to the tack room to finish what he'd started.

"You need help?" Randall asked as he passed where Sawyer was working to get the stalls cleaned out and ready for their occupants.

"Shit," Sawyer swore as the stall door fell off its hinges, nearly landing on his foot. "Just the fuck what I needed."

Randall knelt down. "The hinge gave way. You got fresh ones?"

"Yeah."

"Then let's take the door off so it doesn't break the other one and we can fix it. Get on the other side and we can lift together." Sawyer huffed but did as he asked, and they got the door off and set it aside. "Where are the hinges?"

"In the equipment shed where we put that piece of furniture you wanted to keep."

"Then I'll hold the door while you get what we need," Randall offered, and Sawyer stepped away and hurried out of the barn. Randall looked around and sighed. How in the heck had he let himself get roped into all this? He had plenty that he needed to do back home. The estate manager could handle the day-to-day running of the tours and the boutique, but the rest of the estate required someone to watch over it. He had plans for the grounds that needed to be overseen. He also had an idea to add a distillery to the property. They had crops they were selling, but he figured that some of them could be used to create an estate whiskey they could sell to the visitors, and if they got the mix right, it might even become known beyond the immediate area. Instead, he was here and….

"I found one," Sawyer said as he strode toward him, and Randall momentarily forgot about all the things back home, swallowing hard as the cowboy drew closer.

"Great," Randall said quickly. Sawyer had also brought tools, and they got the old hinge parts removed and the new ones installed. Then came the hard part: sliding the stall door back into place. "Lift it from the other side."

"I have it," Sawyer said, moving the door too far his way. Randall tried to guide it back and the bottom slipped in, but the top hinge missed. "We need to lift it again."

"Okay. I'll lift and you guide," Randall suggested. Sawyer grew quiet, and Randall held the door. "Which way do I go?" He was still quiet, tapping his hand on the gate. Randall began to lower the door simply because his arms were getting tired.

"Not yet. I almost got it." Sawyer finally told him as his arms began to ache.

"Then say something, please," Randall said.

"Just come my way a tiny bit… okay… got it." The door dropped in, and Randall swung it closed and open once more. "That was good." Sawyer patted Randall's shoulder once, which he thought kind of weird.

He wanted to snap that if Sawyer could just talk a little more, it would have been easier. "It's working."

"Yes." He gathered the tools and left without another word. Randall shook his head before returning to the tack room. Bloody hell, he had things to do, and working with Sawyer was a recipe for frustration. He went back to the boring, repetitive task and finished cleaning and oiling the leather. He heard Sawyer working in the stalls, but he stayed where he was, glad to be away from the hot but silent cowboy. Once he was done, Randall left the tack room and the barn, trying to find George and Alan, but they must have been out with the cattle. No one was around the house, and he didn't want to ask Sawyer what was up.

"Hey," Alan's brother Chip said as he ambled across the yard. Didn't anyone just walk here? No. They all moved like they had all the confidence in the world.

"I was looking for Alan," Randall said, feeling more than a little out of sorts. At home he would know exactly what to do, but here he was the outsider. The ranch had horses, just like the estate, but things were done differently here.

"You need something to do?"

Randall groaned before he could stop himself. "What I need is to be away from Sawyer." Blast, he should have kept that to himself.

Chip nodded. "I see."

"I doubt you do." He couldn't help wondering what Chip's sly look meant. "I swear he expects me to read his mind."

He shrugged. "We cowboys are strange. Well, technically I'm a cowboy. I tend cattle and drive them to where we need them to go. I don't do rodeo, though. Mama would have a fit. Mostly I care for our animals. I'm going to be a vet, but that's a long way off yet." He was the most open person Randall had met yet.

"So why aren't you like the rest of them? All tall, dark, and broody." That was Sawyer to a tee. "I don't get the not-talking thing."

"You learn to read between the lines. Besides, these are men of action. They communicate by what they do, not so much in what they say." Chip seemed to scan the horizon and then shrugged. "Hey, Sawyer," Chip called, and Randall groaned as he came over. "Are any of the horses saddled?"

"I can get some ready."

"Then saddle up two. You and Randall here can ride out and see if the guys need help. He should see what we do and how we manage the herds." Sawyer's eyes widened, but he nodded once. "Thanks. I appreciate it. I have to check on Mary Jane. She's about to have her pups at any time, and I don't want her to be alone. She had trouble last time, and I told Mama she shouldn't have any more pups." He sighed. "She got pregnant again before I could have the vet take care of her," he added to Randall. "Go and see what they're doing." He hurried off toward one of the outbuildings, and Randall sighed, following Sawyer into the barn to help him saddle the horses.

At least this was something he was familiar with, and once the horses were ready, he mounted and followed Sawyer out of the yard. God, for the first time since he arrived, he felt comfortable. Horses he understood, and as he rode, he gently patted the chestnut gelding's neck. He was a fine animal and one Randall would be really proud to have in his barn.

Sawyer rode in silence. "I have to ask," Randall finally said, getting tired of the quiet. "Do you ever say much?"

"No," Sawyer told him.

"Really? You just do the strong silent thing."

Sawyer shrugged. "Ain't got a lot to say." Randall rolled his eyes. "You seem to like talking."

"There's something civilized in being able to hold a conversation. I was trained by my nanny to be able to hold a conversation with anyone about just about anything."

Sawyer pulled his horse to a stop. "You had classes in how to talk to people?" He seemed shocked and looked at Randall, shaking his head like he was completely strange.

"Because in my world, you need to know how to act around others. My parents used to have grand parties with dinner for twenty people. I had to know how to speak to the person on my left and my right as well as hold my own in a general conversation. Sometimes the conversation would be about the weather, which was boring, or the economic impact of sanctions in Iran."

Sawyer scoffed and started his horse forward. "Why would you want to talk about that?"

"It's polite to speak about things the guest wishes to talk about. And if you have diplomats at your table, they will talk about their postings and current events and issues. You have to know how to sound interested even when you're bored stiff. Because it's polite. And I had to learn how to do that."

Sawyer didn't slow down, looking toward the horizon. "Is that what you're doing now? Being polite?"

Randall chuckled. "Maybe a little, because manners are always called for. That's another lesson from nanny: manners never go out of style." He sighed. "God, you should have seen the list of rules I had to grow up with." He paused as they crested a rise. The land spread out in front of them, dotted by cattle with men on horseback gathering them. "What are they doing?"

"Cattle are herd animals, so they feel comfortable together and will move as a group. The trick is to get the lead animal moving the way you want them, and the rest will follow. Alan, George, and the other men are relocating them so they don't overgraze the land." He pointed. "See the fence over there and that open gate? It's where they're going to get the herd to get through. Let's go see if they need help." That had to be the most Sawyer had said to him so far.

"Okay. Lead on."

Sawyer spurred his horse forward, and Randall did the same, hurrying toward the others, the land flying beneath them. Few things in life were as exhilarating as riding like the wind.

They slowed as they approached the others. "Glad you're here. We could use you," Alan said. "We've got the main herd, but there are a dozen head back that way maybe a mile."

"We can get them," Sawyer said, tilting his head in that direction and taking off, with Randall following behind. He loved this kind of riding. The open air, the sense of freedom. There was something primal about the team of man and horse. It made his spirits soar. He spurred his horse on faster, giving him his head, passing Sawyer like he was standing still. He laughed as Sawyer tried to catch up, but he had too much of a head start.

"You can do it," he whispered, urging the horse to a full-on gallop, loving the power under him. When he saw the cattle ahead, he pulled up, bringing his horse to a walk.

"You ride good," Sawyer said when he caught up.

"I wanted to be a jockey when I was a boy. My father wouldn't have it and said I was to be a solicitor instead. He said it was what the family needed. So that was what I did." Nothing gave him the thrill a horse did, though. Randall checked out the small group of cattle gathered near the water. "What do we do?"

Sawyer turned to him just as his horse neighed in panic, rearing back. Randall moved his horse away and jumped off. What the fuck was going on?

Sawyer's horse stomped and reared again as Randall tried to see what was happening. "It's a snake." Or what was left of one. The horse's hooves had squashed it.

Sawyer backed his horse away and then Randall hurried over, speaking softly. Sawyer somehow managed to stay on the panicked beast as it continued stomping. "It's okay. The snake is dead," he said softly. At least the horse stayed on four legs, and Randall continued speaking softly. Huge ears turned toward him, straining to hear as Randall took the reins, patting the horse's neck. "It's okay." He held the horse still, and Sawyer dismounted.

"That was something," he said, and Randall gave him a serious look.

"A snake startled him. It's been squashed, and we need to calm him so he doesn't bolt." He kept his voice low and calm. "That's a good boy." He patted the horse's neck and then handed the reins to Sawyer before returning to his own horse and calming him as well. "Are you all right? Did you get hurt?" Sawyer shook his head. "Staying on him was impressive."

"I knew if I fell off that I was likely to get stomped," Sawyer told him, and Randall agreed.

"Let's give them a few minutes to calm down," Randall offered before moving his horse away from the snake carcass. It wasn't moving, but he didn't need the horse to try to bolt. He was still breathing hard. Sawyer followed with his horse, and the walk did them all good. "Then we can get the cattle."

Sawyer nodded, and they continued forward, approaching the cattle. Randall remounted, breathing deeply to calm himself, and Sawyer did the same, taking a wide look around the small group before calling out to get them moving. It took a little maneuvering, but they eventually got the head moving in the right direction.

CHAPTER 4

"I HEARD what you did," Chip said to Randall as they all arrived back in the yard. The sun was setting, and Sawyer was exhausted. He had been ill at ease since his horse tried to bolt, and he was damned lucky Randall had been there and knew what to do. Otherwise, it was likely he would have been dumped, stomped, and stranded in the middle of nowhere.

"It was nothing," Randall said, which rankled Sawyer. As though potentially saving his life meant nothing.

"I wouldn't say that," Chip said. "Remember that town is over ten miles away, and you were well over a mile from anyone else. If Sawyer had been hurt, it would have taken a long time to get help. People can die out here." He was so serious, and Randall nodded slowly.

"Then I'm just glad I could help," Randall said softly. "I've spent a lot of time around horses."

"I didn't know that," George said. "I thought your family had given up much of their livestock."

"My father did. He sold most of our breeding stock when I was a teenager. He said it was too expensive for not enough reward. Then he turned the stables into the gift shop and tea house for the tourists. I have two horses on the estate now, and that's it."

Alan shrugged. "That's really sad. Why would he do that? Even I know that you used to breed top-notch racers."

Randall blinked and his cheeks reddened, but he remained still, glancing around.

"We need to get the horses unsaddled and watered," Sawyer said and led the horses away. Judging by the fact that the usually talkative Randall was suddenly really quiet, he needed a way to get away from the gossip. "They did good."

"Yes, they did." Randall followed him, and once the horses were in their stalls, Randall worked to unsaddle his mount, speaking quietly to the horse.

Sawyer shook his head at his big brown-eyed beast. "You really had me scared there for a while," he told the horse, unfastening the girth and pulling off the saddle and blanket. "But you did good work nonetheless." He patted his neck before combing him out and checking his hooves. Then he made sure he had plenty of water and hay as well as some oats before leaving the stall. He met Randall as he headed to the tack room to put everything away.

"Did your father really sell the horses?" Sawyer asked. Randall nodded. "Was it because you wanted to be a jockey?"

Randall nodded once more. "He had definite plans for me, and he made sure they came to pass. He also made quite a bit of money off the deal, and what he did is still helping to pay for the upkeep of the estate." He made it sound logical, but Sawyer figured there was a lot more to it. It was none of his business. A man was entitled to his own thoughts and his own counsel. He didn't need others butting in.

Sawyer finished putting everything away, his stomach growling. Then he made sure that all the horses were bedded down for the night before leaving the barn. "It's time for dinner." He closed up and went in to eat, grateful it wasn't his turn to cook.

SAWYER LAY in his room in the bunkhouse, on his side, trying to sleep. He knew he shouldn't let this uppity earl get to him, but he kept thinking about what a pain in the ass the man was and yet how he hadn't thought twice before saving Sawyer's butt out there. He turned over again, trying not to visualize those eyes or the hurt in them when he'd told Sawyer about his father.

Sawyer knew firsthand what it was like to live with a father who wanted to control everything, including his wife and son. He pulled the blankets up to his neck, trying to stop the shiver that went through him. *He is not here, and I'm free of him.* Sawyer told himself that over and over in order to calm the jitters that took over whenever he thought of the old asshole. It had taken a long time before he didn't think about what he had done to him, how his father had made his life miserable. He took deep breaths and clamped his eyes closed, bringing up better memories, like the ones he'd made working here, where he was valued.

He tried to sleep, but the clock next to the bed showed almost midnight. He got up and quietly left the room, intending to get a drink of water. A single light shone in the small living area. He peered down to find Harley sitting in a chair reading. He was one of the hands that had been on the ranch for years. "Did I wake you?" Harley asked, setting his book aside. "Sometimes I can't sleep, so I get up and read."

"No. You were fine. I can't sleep either." He got his drink of water and intended to go back to bed. "Too many things to think about."

"You can't let what happened today bother you. It's happened to all of us. Horses are creatures, and they have minds of their own. They're both strong and delicate, and they get startled. It had nothing to do with you." Leave it to Harley to have a sensible view of things.

"It's not that, but thank you." He sat down and put his feet up. "My mind keeps churning around and around, and I can't get it to stop." He sighed and wished he could settle down. He had to be up at six and had a full day ahead. He should be exhausted after the day he'd had, but he was still wide-awake.

"You could try reading or something. I sometimes watch television, but that would probably keep the guys up," he said softly before handing Sawyer a book.

"*Moby Dick*?" he asked.

"Yeah. It's long and drawn out. There's a good story, but I bet after less than an hour, it will put you to sleep." He smiled, and Sawyer opened the book and began to read. Sure enough, after about twenty pages, he was struggling to stay awake. He set the book aside, returning to his room. This time when he closed his eyes, he managed to keep his mind from whirring and finally fell asleep.

AFTER DRESSING and coffee, Sawyer went to the barn and turned out the horses. He had slept late without meaning to, but was grateful that Randall hadn't come out yet. Though he wasn't actually sure he was going to. It was always possible that Alan had assigned him somewhere else.

"The three colts should be arriving in a couple of hours," Mrs. Justice told him as he closed one of the stall doors. He hadn't even heard her coming.

"All right. Do you want to see the stalls? I have them ready." He took her back to where fresh bedding awaited the new arrivals.

"Excellent."

"And I thought we could put them out in the paddock together. There's enough room, and they shouldn't bother each other too much."

She nodded. "I agree, and once they get settled, you can start training them. All three horses are blank slates, so I want to train them right. And we have plenty of time. I'm not interested in breaking these horses. I want to start them. Get them used to us and working with people. That way once they're ready for the saddle, they'll take it easily."

"What sort of training are you interested in?"

"All three of these horses should be cutters, but you know how things go. Some horses don't work out the way their breeding says they should. So we'll start there and let the colts tell us where their strengths are."

"Sounds good to me." Sawyer waited to see if she had anything else before returning to work. He finished getting the stalls set up with hay and water. The rest of the horses were out in their paddocks, so it was a good time to get those stalls spot cleaned and fresh bedding laid down. "Is Randall coming out?" he asked before she left.

"He went with George and Alan this morning."

Sawyer nodded and turned away. It was time to get the job done and stop letting his attention wander to Randall. What he really needed to do was get the man out of his head, and the easiest way to do that was to spend as much time away from him as possible. Sawyer should have been happy not to work with Randall today. Why was he disappointed instead?

ALAN, GEORGE, Chip, and Randall leaned on the paddock fence later that afternoon, watching the horses. "These are the new colts?" George asked with a smile. "They look great."

"I thought so," Sawyer said, setting the pitchfork aside before joining them. Thankfully his work was finished for the day, and he could finally take a breather. "They're just settling in and finding their way around. It will take some time before they're ready for any kind of training."

"Mom has a really good eye," Chip agreed as more of the men gathered to watch the young horses. They frolicked and chased one another around the paddock. It was a great thing to see, and Sawyer found himself smiling as he leaned against the fence, almost touching Randall, but not quite. There weren't many times when everything seemed to grind to a halt, not on a ranch, but this was one of them. The new horses captured everyone's attention. Sawyer turned to find a smile on Randall's face, and it stayed in place when he looked at him, the two of them sharing the contentment of one of the simple joys of life.

These moments never lasted long enough, and the crunch of tires on the gravel drive pulled Sawyer's attention. An old, dented truck with spots of rust marring the faded black paint came to a stop near the barn. The others turned as well. Alan pushed away from the fence. "Can I help you?" he asked as he strode toward the truck.

A voice Sawyer had hoped he'd never hear again answered just as he turned back to the colts. Instantly, he straightened, tightness forming in his belly and running down his back. "Who is that?" Randall asked from next to him.

Sawyer swallowed and slowly turned around, staring at the barrel-chested man with gray hair and stone-cold eyes. "My father," he answered, the words turning to chalk in his mouth. As much as he wanted to turn and walk away, he knew he couldn't leave Alan or anyone else on the ranch to deal with the old bastard. "What do you want?" he asked as he approached.

"Is that any way to greet your old man? I haven't seen you in—"

"Four years and three months," Sawyer spat. "So I'll ask again, what do you want?" He refused to turn away from him. Sawyer was no longer a child, and even though years of conditioning tried to kick in, he refused to let them take hold.

"Do you want us to make him leave?" Randall asked from right next to him. He hadn't even realized he was there. "We will if that's what you want." He wasn't loud, but the force in his voice gave Sawyer strength.

"No. I just want to know why he's here." He never took his gaze off the man. He didn't dare.

"Can't a father stop in to say hello to his son?" his father asked in a gentle tone that Sawyer knew was completely false and only for the benefit of the others around.

"They can, but *you* don't. You want something, so you may as well spit it out." He clenched his fists and then released them.

"Why don't we give them a chance to talk?" Alan said, guiding the others away.

Sawyer was grateful. The last thing he wanted was to have an audience for a conversation with his POS father.

"Fine. We can talk in the barn," Sawyer said, leading his father out of the yard. At first Randall held back, but Sawyer turned toward him, and Randall followed.

"I'd like to speak to my son alone," his father said to Randall, who folded his arms over his chest, doing his best imitation of a cowboy.

"And I'd like to be a prince of the realm, but that isn't going to happen either." Damn, his accent came out even more when he used his formal drawing-room voice. "It's clear that Sawyer doesn't want to speak to you or see you, so it's best that there is a witness."

Sawyer cleared his throat.

"Who's the uppity fella?"

"Oh," Sawyer said. "That's Randall. He's the Earl of Plymouth, apparently. The man who suggested we speak privately is married to the Duke of Northumberland." He flashed a quick smile. "Yeah. You wandered into the part of Wyoming that's just chock full of cowboy nobility. Tell me what you want so I can go back to my life and you can get the hell out of here."

"You owe me, boy." There was the tone he was used to. "I brought you into this world…."

"And what?" Randall snapped. "You think you can threaten him?" Damn, he drew himself upward.

"It's all right," Sawyer said as levelly as he could. "He's come all this way for nothing. What happened—did you lose your job?" He saw his father flinch ever so slightly and knew he'd gotten it in one. "And now he needs money. Well, he isn't getting any of mine." He was staring at him and ready for a reaction, but he still didn't see the slap coming. Sawyer took a step back, his cheek stinging. "Dammit," he said with a scowl, turning back just as his father went down to his knees.

"You treat your son better than that, you stupid git," Randall swore, hitting Sawyer's father with an uppercut that sent him back into a sprawl on the concrete. "Get up if you want more, because I'll be happy to give it to you."

"What the fuck?" Alan demanded as he raced inside.

"He hit Sawyer, so I took care of the problem," Randall said as through he'd just put his dishes in the sink. Like this was a normal day and he hadn't just taken down Sawyer's much bigger father. "I think this man has had enough and it's time for him to go. Maybe drive him toward town and toss him in a gutter, where he belongs."

Alan seemed amused. "All right. What do you want, Sawyer?"

"Him to be gone." Sawyer's cheek still stung, along with his pride. He hated that his father had treated him that way, but even more, he hated that others had seen his weakness. That made him wish a hole would open up and swallow him.

Chapter 5

Randall seethed. Hell, he had no idea where this protective instinct had come from. When Sawyer's father hit him, Randall had seen red and reacted without thinking about it. No one should hit someone else like that.

He grabbed Sawyer's father and yanked him to his feet, with Alan on the other side. They half poured him into his truck. "Have you been drinking?" Alan asked, wrinkling his nose.

"What the fuck, man? I got a right to talk to my kid."

"Not if Sawyer doesn't want to speak to you," Randall snapped, yanking away the keys once he fished them out of his pocket. "Alan, call the police. He's driving while under the influence." He was furious and wanted to teach this asshole a lesson.

"Please," Sawyer said, "let him sober up awhile and then get him out of here. The police will only make him stick around, and I want him on his way back to whatever corner of hell he came from."

"All right," Alan said. "Go on back to work, all of you. I got this." He turned back to Sawyer's father, and Sawyer hurried into the barn. Randall thought about going after him, but Chip took his arm and held him back.

"He needs some time on his own," he cautioned.

Randall stood still, watching as Sawyer disappeared inside. He wanted to talk to him, but then thought better of it. Maybe Chip was right and Sawyer needed time. But that was so counter to Randall's nature that he nearly followed him anyway. "Bollocks."

Chip chuckled. "Yeah. I can agree with that."

Alan still stood next to the truck, with Sawyer's father lounging inside, looking about to fall asleep. "Come on. I have the cure for everything sad." Chip hurried away, and Randall had to rush to keep up.

Chip slipped into one of the small outbuildings off to the back of the yard. Inside, Randall found him smiling as a black dog with a white stripe on her nose lay on her side, nursing a litter of wriggling pups. "This is Mary Jane. And that is her last litter of puppies. I'm having her spayed after this. She's getting older, and I don't want the poor girl to have any more." He gently patted her head. "You're a good mama." She panted, and Chip hurried away, then returned with some water and a few treats.

"What are those?"

"I make up bites with a little chicken, some rice, and a few supplements. She loves them, and with the pups, it's hard for her to get enough to eat, so I feed these to her a few times a day. She's a special girl. George rescued her and her mama, Daisy, when he first got here. He found them in a culvert. When we first met George, we didn't know who he was. But he needed help, and he came with Daisy and her four pups. I knew he was a good man back then. Alan didn't trust him, but that soon changed." Chip snickered.

"Is Daisy still here?"

Chip shook his head. "She passed away last year. Archie, Mary Jane's brother, is in England. George and Alan took him back with them a while ago. I got to see him the last time I visited, and he's a daddy too. Really beautiful dog." Chip sighed as the puppies wriggled and jostled each other. He reached down and gently picked one up. Its eyes were still closed, and Chip held the pup so gently. It yawned and curled up in Chip's hands. "You're going to grow up big and strong."

"Do you give them aspirations?" Randall asked.

Chip shrugged. "I guess I tell them what I hope. They are cute pups, and their mother is good at the ranch, so they should be. I'll put the word out that I have them, and folks will give them good homes. I want to keep one, but Mom isn't convinced yet."

Randall smiled. "Let me guess. You always want to keep one."

"Nope," Chip said smugly. "I always want to keep two, but I figure I can wear Mom down to one. It is a ranch, after all, and I care for them."

"Yeah, but what about when you go back to school?"

"Then the local vet steps in for me. He and I have a deal. I help him out when I'm on breaks, and he gives me practical experience. I've still got a long ways to go, but this is what I want."

"It seems like a hard life out here," Randall said, thinking about evenings spent in his library with a book, a glass of whiskey or brandy, and a warm fire. His life in England was very settled, and he liked it that way. He didn't live extravagantly, but instead comfortably.

"Maybe. But this is a good way to live." He put the pup back with its mother, and the little thing nuzzled right in to eat some more. "I've been to England. Spent a month there with Alan and George the last few years. It's really pretty there, and everyone was nice, but it wasn't home." He backed away from Mary Jane and her pups, leaving them alone, and then stepped outside. "Look up there, at those mountains. It's still wild. There are wolves and bears, but no people. That's all federal land, and it's just left on its own. There's something thrilling about that." He paused. "Have you heard any wolves at night? I did maybe a week ago, but not since. The dogs that are out with the herds answered and warned them off."

"How do you know?"

"Because I was out there and I heard them. They were quite a ways away, and the dogs gave their warnings. After that the wolves were quiet. We had troubles with wolves a few years ago. They attacked a few of the calves, but Alan added the dogs in with the herd. That really seemed to make a difference." Chip sighed. "He wanted to kill the wolves, but I convinced him to try the dogs first."

"But they affected your family's livelihood?" Randall asked. He would have expected them to take Alan's more aggressive approach.

"Yeah, but wolves are good for the environment. Not so good for the cattle, but they keep the deer and other herd animal populations under control. They're part of the food chain, and the more people try to mess with that, the more damage we do because of unintended consequences. Yeah, we want to get rid of the wolves, but then the deer and other animal populations grow and they eat everything, so the woods don't get a chance to grow and mature with the grazers eating all the new growth. It just keeps going. Alan doesn't agree with me, but he's gone most of the time, and Mom and I worked it out."

"Your mother is…." He didn't quite have the words. She was an amazingly strong person.

"A force of nature?" Chip asked, and Randall nodded. "What is your mom like?" Chip asked. "Is she a countess?"

"She was. My mom was every bit the countess, but in a good way. She always thought that her title meant she had to use it for the benefit of everyone else. Mom was always raising money to help the village or pushing for some sort of project. She was a lot like your mom in some ways. But she died when I was fourteen." Then everything changed. He always wished his mother had spent as much time with him as she had with her causes.

"I'm sorry." Chip sighed. "I don't know what I'd do without my mom, especially after Dad died."

Randall nodded. "Losing a parent is tough." Though both of his were gone, he didn't mourn his father the way he had his mother. His father became harsh and unmoving in his grief. Maybe he'd always been that way and his mother had mitigated it—Randall didn't know. But his one major regret was not getting to know his mother as an adult.

"Do you think Sawyer's dad is still here?" Chip asked as he went to the door. Randall followed, and Sawyer came out of the barn. He took one look at the truck and headed over to where they stood, pointedly ignoring the vehicle and its inhabitant. "That was pretty cool what you did. How did you learn to fight like that?" Sawyer stood next to Chip.

"I was a gay kid in a British boarding school. I learned to fight quickly, and I got really good at it. All I had to do was take down one kid and the others left me alone. I took down one of the bullies right in front of the headmaster. He pulled me into his office, and I thought I was in big trouble." He swallowed, remembering the panic he'd felt at the time. If he had been kicked out of school, his father would have been over-the-house angry, and Randall would have paid for it.

"Did you get a beating?" Sawyer asked. "Like on TV?"

Randall shook his head. "The headmaster sat me down and asked what happened. When I told him, he gave me a cup of tea and said to stay where I was for a little while and calm down."

"Jesus, do you all have a tea for everything?" Sawyer asked.

"Well, yes, we do, actually. There are teas to wake you up, some to help you sleep. There are ones served at society functions as well as afternoon tea, which is like a snack time rather than just tea. But in this case, the headmaster just wanted me to calm down."

"Did he expel you?" Chip asked.

"No. He didn't beat me either. The other boys all thought I got punished, and I just smiled to cover it up. But the bully never bothered me again. Or any of the other boys, for that matter."

"But my father," Sawyer began and then stopped.

"What?" Randall asked. "Is a bully? I've met plenty of those in my life, and I know how to handle them. Besides, the guy was half drunk."

Chip looked at each of them and then nodded before striding toward the house.

"Why did you do that?"

"Do what?"

"Take him on," Sawyer asked. "Why'd you hit him? I don't remember anyone ever taking him on that way."

"Maybe it's something that someone should have done a long time ago. And as for why, I saw him hit you and I just acted on instinct. It wasn't something I thought about." And he didn't intend to ponder the reasons behind it either. He wasn't a violent person by nature. But…. He needed to change the subject. "Is your father sobering up?"

"Alan doesn't want him to go anywhere for an hour or so," Sawyer said. "So I'm stuck with him sitting out there, and I don't want to talk to him, but there he is."

"Then let's go," Randall offered. "I need to go into town for a few things, and you can get away at the same time."

Some of Sawyer's tension seemed to ease out of him. "Yeah, let's do that. I'll let Alan know." He hurried away, and Randall went inside to see about borrowing one of the ranch trucks.

IN THE end, he let Sawyer drive. Randall wasn't used to driving on the wrong side of the road. Even sitting on this side of the truck, he kept reaching for the gear shift. He stopped himself most of the time, but as they approached Covington, another truck pulled in front of them. Sawyer pressed the brakes hard, and without thinking, Randall reached for the gear shift, gripping Sawyer's warm hand. He immediately looked over and got a glance in return. The thing was, he forgot to remove his hand. Slowly he pulled it back. "Sorry," he muttered and turned to look out the window so Sawyer didn't see the way he blushed like a schoolboy over his first crush.

Sawyer pulled into a diagonal parking space in front of The General's Mercantile. He looked at the sign more than once, trying to parse it. "It's a play on words. The store was started by a general a long time ago."

"Got it." He followed Sawyer inside, wondering if he'd stepped back in time about sixty years. The merchandise seemed current, but the building was a time warp, with old-fashioned shelves and pictures on the walls that must have been there for decades.

Randall picked up a few pairs of jeans, trying to figure out his size. Sawyer pulled them out of his hands, put them back, and passed him a different pair. "Cowboys wear these," he muttered.

"So I'm a cowboy now?"

Sawyer's gaze held his for a few seconds. Randall wasn't sure if he was sizing him up, trying to figure out if he was joking, or about ready to cut him to ribbons. "Not yet. But maybe someday." He turned away, and Randall checked out the jeans. He held them up to himself, and damned if they didn't seem to be the right size.

"How'd you do that?"

"Cowboys know jeans." Again, very little response.

Randall got a second pair and continued through the store. Sawyer tossed a couple shirts his way. They were heavy… and plaid, which wasn't his thing. But when he went to put them back, he got almost a growl, so he held on to them.

"Boots," Sawyer said and led him over. He showed Randall the selection and thankfully let him pick out his own. Apparently they were all acceptable. Finally, with a mountain of stuff in his hands, Sawyer led him to the hats and crossed his arms. Apparently this was some sort of test, because there was no indication of any kind. There were white hats, buff ones, darker brown, and even black. He knew he was going to look like a cowboy ghost if he picked the white one, but the buff ones looked nice, so he picked one up and checked it in the mirror. It didn't look bad, but it wasn't right. He put it back and gently lifted another. This hat had a dark leather band, and when he put it on, there might have been a hint of a smile from Sawyer.

"Can I help you?" a kid asked as he hurried up. "You need to get the right size."

"This one seems to fit," Randall said, but the kid shook his head. "All right."

The kid took the hat when he offered it and put it back. Then he hurried away and returned with a hat box. "That's Peter. His family has run this store for generations."

Peter set down the box and pulled out the hat. "Try this one." He smiled eagerly, and Randall put the hat on his head. "It sits a little lower, so it isn't going to fly off when you ride or in the wind." He seemed pleased, and the hat felt good.

"Thank you, Peter," Randall said.

"You must be one of Alan and George's friends." He flashed a toothy grin. "If you want me to take your stuff, I can put it at the counter." When Randall nodded, he hurried away, like it was impossible for him to sit still. Then he was back. "Can I help you with anything else?" he asked with another grin.

"No. Thank you. I think I'll just look around."

Peter nodded briskly before turning to Sawyer. "I heard you guys got some new colts. Will you be training them? Can I come see them?"

"Yes. Come on out whenever your mama says you can. I'll be training them in a few weeks, and you can help on Sundays if your mama says it's okay."

"Thanks, Mr. Sawyer," he said, hurrying away with all that energy going in every direction.

"I take it he likes horses," Randall said.

Sawyer hummed and began looking through the store. Randall got the idea there was a story there, but he didn't figure that Sawyer was going to tell him what it was. Sawyer's phone rang, and he answered it, then humphed once before saying thanks and hanging up. "Alan let my father drive away. He seemed okay."

"That's good. At least he'll be gone," Randall said, but all he got in response was a look cold enough to freeze water in July. "Okay...." He excused himself and continued looking through the store, picking up a few things he needed as well as some snacks. One of the things he craved was crisps, and they had a whole section of salty snacks. He got a few small bags of the kinds he thought he'd like and then took everything to the counter, where Peter rang him up. Randall put it all on his card. Peter bagged everything except the boots and hat, and then took care of Sawyer.

"Thanks for your help," Randall told Peter before they left the store. They stowed their purchases in the truck. "You hungry?" Some amazing scents drifted across the road, making his stomach rumble. Sawyer shrugged. "You have to smell that."

Sawyer nodded, and Randall headed across the road to the weirdest amalgamation of a building he had ever seen. The sign out front read simply Roy's. He couldn't figure out if it was a bar or a restaurant and maybe a hotel. Turned out it was all three, and the spicy, smoky scents coming from the dining room pulled him right in.

The inside was as rustic as the outside, with scarred tables and floors that had probably seen just about everything. "I don't think this is a good idea."

"Why?" Randall asked.

Sawyer tilted his head to the side. "Those men over there are the hands at one of the other ranches. There's an old rivalry and bad feelings because they wanted to get their hands on some of the land that is now part of the ranch. It's a long story. Tank and Collin know the whole of it. I only heard some of the gossip, but I got enough of it to know that their boss is still pretty pissed, and I don't want any trouble."

"So you aren't going to eat here?" Randall asked. "No way. We'll keep to ourselves, and they can do the same." He was hungry and sat down at one of the tables a good distance from the others.

"What can I getcha?" a server asked as she slid plastic-coated menus in front of them. She leaned closer, her strong perfume nearly making Randall sneeze. "Looks like you two got the natives restless."

"Maybe we should go."

"Sawyer, you stay right there. If they cause trouble, I'll have Roy kick them out of here fast." She winked. "They tip for shit and always cause trouble. Now, the brisket is to die for today." She glared at the group of men, and they all lowered their gazes.

"Thanks. That sounds delicious," Randall said with a smile.

"Well, isn't your accent just delightful," she said, her smile widening.

"Sally," Sawyer said, his eyes darkening and hers widening.

Sally's smile dimmed. "Oh, I see. He's yours," she said. "Well, far be it from me to poach anyone, but sugar, you are one sweet-lookin' man." She sighed. "You each want a beer?"

Randall ordered a soda, and Sawyer did the same. Then Sally hurried away, and Randall leaned over the table. "What was all that about?"

"Sally is always on the lookout," Sawyer explained.

"I'm not talking about her, but you? If I didn't know better I'd say that you liked me." He was teasing, but the way Sawyer sputtered for just a second told him he had hit the nail on the head. "Well, that's an interesting bit of information."

Sawyer snorted. "You don't know shit about nothing."

"Yeah, then why are your eyes so dark? And you're sweating. I also see the way you watch me." Randall leaned closer so he could speak more softly.

"What are you doing here?" a gruff voice asked, and Randall turned and looked into the eyes of Sawyer's father. Bloody hell.

Chapter 6

Sawyer wanted to sink through the floor. Just when he thought he had gotten rid of the man, he showed up again. "I could ask you the same thing." He turned away.

"Did you think you could get rid of me so easily?"

"I suggest you go, and this time leave town," Randall said. "Remember what I did before. I can certainly take care of you again."

"I'm not drunk this time."

Randall stood. "So I won't go easy on you. This time, you won't be walking anywhere. Now, turn around, stop bullying your son, and go." He sounded so reasonable.

"Where did they dig you up from anyway? Are you an extra in a movie or something?" He smiled. "You aren't really the earl of whatever it was."

"Actually, I am. I inherited the title from my father."

"You need to go," Sawyer told his father. "I'm not going to give you anything, not even the time of day."

Sally came over to the table. "Is he joining you?" she asked.

"No. He's leaving, and you might want to get someone to escort him to the door. He's here to cause trouble." Randall sat down. "Thank you for your assistance, Sally. I really appreciate it."

"You better go. Sawyer and the British hottie are welcome here; you… not so much." She pointed to the door. "Don't make me get help. You will regret it." Sawyer's father leered at her, and Sawyer wondered if he was going to take a swing at someone, but he left and headed to the door. It slammed after him, and Sally refilled their glasses. "Your food will be out soon."

"Thank you," Sawyer said. "For helping."

She snorted. "My father was a real SOB too. I know how to handle assholes like him…." She pointed toward the other guys. "And them."

"Thanks, Sally."

"No problem, sweetie," she said before patting his shoulder. Then she headed to the kitchen, returning with plates that she set in front of each of them.

"What's your father's issue?" Randall asked.

"Gambling. He can never seem to stop. And he isn't very good at it. He loses a lot more than he wins, and he always needs money. It's why my mother left him, and now he thinks that I'll be able to bail him out of whatever mess he's got himself into." Sawyer took a bite, humming at the spicy warmth in the beef.

Randall set down his fork and wiped the corners of his mouth. "What kind of people does your father owe?"

Sawyer shrugged. "Probably seedy ones. I really don't know. Why?"

Randall set down his napkin. "Because men like that don't care who they get their money from as long as they get paid. They may be leaning on your father now, but they could come directly to you… or to Alan and George. They don't care who they pressure to get what they want."

It was suddenly very cold. "His issues are his own. They aren't mine or anyone else's."

"And these people aren't exactly law-abiding citizens. They will do whatever they want to get paid." He went back to eating, but Sawyer's appetite suddenly sprouted wings.

"They could come after me?" he asked.

Randall nodded. "A colleague of my father's got himself into trouble and he didn't have the money to pay. They threatened his kids and his wife. They even had pictures of his grandchildren playing in the park. He ended up selling everything, including his house, to pay them. And it isn't like your father cares for anyone other than himself, so he isn't going to care if you get hurt, as long as it keeps the pressure off him."

"So what do we do?"

Randall picked up his fork. "First thing, you eat your lunch, and then when we get back to the ranch, we have a talk with Mrs. Justice and Alan. They have to know what we think is going on so they can alert law enforcement." He slowly ate his lunch, and Sawyer tried to do the same, but now as people entered, he kept wondering if they were coming after him. "Relax for now. We'll figure it out."

"This doesn't have anything to do with you," Sawyer said. "Why would you get involved?"

"Because I'm not as callous as you seem to think I am." He smiled slightly, and Sawyer nodded.

"Thanks." Stopping him from getting hit by his father was one thing, but putting himself on the line with guys like this… that was something else. "I was thinking that maybe it's best if I move on. I've been here on the ranch for some time, but if I take off, then no one else needs to get in the middle of this shit with my father."

Randall shook his head. "First thing, the family is going to miss you, and secondly, these guys have people who specialize in finding folks. If they want you, they will figure out where you are. The best thing to do is tell everyone what you think. A united front is a lot stronger than you on your own." He gently set down his fork. "Now go ahead and eat. This is too good to let go to waste." He continued eating, and Sawyer forced himself to finish. Randall paid the bill when they were done.

"Thanks, Sally."

"This was amazing," Randall told her as she cleared away the plates. "I've never had this kind of cooking before." He gave her a good tip, and they headed to the truck, then drove out of town and back to the ranch.

"WHAT'S GOING on?" Alan asked as he, George, Chip, Mrs. Justice, Claude—back from a trip to Dallas—and Randall all sat in the living room of the main house. Claude and Mrs. J held hands as they sat on the sofa, glancing at each other gently.

"Just tell us what's on your mind," Mrs. Justice said. "We'll deal with it."

Sawyer swallowed hard. "That's just it. You shouldn't have to."

"Is this about your dad?" Chip interrupted.

"Yeah. You know he came here wanting money. Well, Dad has a gambling problem. He always has. Can't stay away from casinos, horses, dog tracks, you name it. There were times when I was growing up that he'd gamble away the food money." He really didn't want to think about those times and how the only food he got all day was lunch at school. "And when he lost, he got mean."

"And Sawyer thinks his father owes the wrong people money," Randall explained. Sawyer was grateful that he didn't have to say it. "And it's possible that could put him as well as the people here in danger."

Mrs. Justice picked up the phone, dialed, and within seconds was speaking to the sheriff. "I need you out at the ranch, Johnny." She sounded like she expected him to jump now. "It's not a crime, no. Not yet." She hung up the phone. "He's on his way."

"Good," Claude said, putting an arm around her as she settled next to him once more. "I can make a few calls to some friends if needed. They run a security firm out of Dallas, and they've protected people against worse folks than gambling debt collectors."

Sawyer nodded. "Thank you. But I don't want to put all of you out like this."

"We look after our own."

"Yes, we do," Alan said. "Look, Sawyer, you need to move into the house. It will be safer, and there are folks close by all the time."

"But—" he began.

"It's a good idea," Randall said. "These kinds of people wait until you're alone and at your most vulnerable. Then they spring themselves on you."

Chip cleared his throat, and Sawyer saw him and Alan exchange glances and darting looks.

"Behave," Mrs. J told them. "Yes. We have room, and you're not to go anywhere alone. And if your father comes back again, we know how to deal with deadbeats. As for his issues, we can see to it that they stay his and don't become yours." She leaned back. "I'm sorry, Randall. When we invited you here, we didn't mean to get you in the middle of a squabble."

"It's not your fault. It's mine," Sawyer said.

Mrs. J leaned forward. "Understand that this is a family matter, and all of the people on this ranch are family. It's how we live and why we are successful. And we look after our own."

"We definitely do," Claude agreed. "There are plenty of people who have your back. Your father is responsible for his own actions and his debts. You are not." He leaned closer for a few seconds, and then the two of them stood and quietly left the room.

"Too bad Tank isn't here. He can scare the crap out of anyone," Chip put in. "But he and Collin are back in England now."

"We'll figure it out." Alan stood and left the room as headlights pulled into the drive.

Sawyer was not at all sure how he felt about everyone knowing his family business and, quite frankly, his shame. He had done his best to try to move beyond that part of his life and wished more than anything that the past would just stay there. He had spent most of his childhood either avoiding his father or dealing with the aftermath of his disasters. His mother had divorced him, and that brought some peace for a while. But the old goat always seemed to find them and put the screws to them, one way or another.

A knock on the door startled him even though he knew the sheriff was on his way. His nerves were strung way too tight. Alan opened it, and the sheriff strode in. He was a middle-aged man who look like he had seen just about everything.

"Your mother called," he said gruffly.

"Knock off the attitude, Johnny," Mrs. J said as she came in the room. "I used to babysit you when you were a kid, and I know things. Remember that." She didn't sit down, but held his gaze until he looked away. Damn, she was something else. "Sawyer has some things that he needs to tell you. And know that I take him seriously, so don't give him any of your usual business."

John Creiton was well known for running a tight ship. "What is it, then?" His tone grew less edgy.

"My father," Sawyer said.

Randall cleared his throat. "We thought it important to tell you that he's been here and was making demands on Sawyer. He didn't get very far."

"I know. I already got a complaint about him and you. Seems there was a bit of a dustup at Roy's. Apparently everyone agrees that he was causing trouble, but I don't like any ill behavior in my town." He glared at both of them.

"Knock it off, Johnny," Mrs. J cut in. "We called you because Sawyer's father has a gambling problem and it's likely some folks are after him for some money. He's trying to get Sawyer to help him." She pursed her lips. "You know what those kinds of men can be like."

"Shit," he said, drawing out the word. "What do you want me to do?"

"Nothing. We just wanted to make sure you knew what was going on. We're all being good citizens here, and I expect you to treat everyone the way you should." The sheriff was known to have issues with guys like Sawyer and Alan.

"I'll do my job."

She stepped forward. "I know you think you will. But it's become known that you take your sweet time answering certain kinds of calls, and that needs to end. Am I making myself clear? Next year is an election year, and there are others who could always step up and decide to run against you." Damn, she had balls of steel, and fuck all if the sheriff didn't take a step back. "You've done good for this town, but you need to help all of it, and not just the ones you think might deserve it."

"Now, Maureen. I didn't take the complaint against Sawyer here seriously. And his friend…." He glanced at Randall. "Well, Sally stood up for him."

"Did you speak with my father?" Sawyer asked.

"I tried to, but I haven't been able to find him yet, and Sally and Roy have decided not to press charges. So there isn't much I can do."

"And he assaulted Sawyer here on the ranch. But we handled it and made him sober up before driving," Alan said. "We stood guard on him."

The sheriff nodded. "I thank you for that." He turned his attention to Sawyer, who expected the third degree. "What did he do?"

"He hit him," Randall answered.

Sawyer nodded. "Randall took him down."

The sheriff humphed. "You ain't that big."

"I know how to handle myself, and I can take care of the people who are important." Damn, Randall's accent was heavy, and he stood tall, speaking to the sheriff in a haughty tone that must be his earl voice. "I should probably introduce myself. Randall Whealton, Earl of Plymouth." Sawyer wanted to snort at the way Randall acted, especially since he had seen him shoveling out horse stalls.

"What the hell is going on? Is half of England over here?"

"He's a friend of mine," George said. "So is Viscount Haferton. You have probably heard about us. We're all part of the family."

The sheriff shook his head like he was trying to figure out if the damned world had turned on its ear. "Okay. Not that any of the fancy titles matter all that much here, but I will look into this as best I can. You call if anything happens. If he shows up here again, call. I can take him in if he causes trouble or if he makes any more threats." He paused. "But do yourselves and me a favor if you can. Try to find out who he owes money to. That will help."

"Thank you, Johnny," Mrs. J said with a smirk. "Alan and Sawyer will see you out." She waited while he and Alan went out with the sheriff.

"Your mother…," the sheriff began.

"Yeah, I know. But she looks after everyone the same way she looked after us. This is her home—our home—and you know us cowboys and cowgirls." They protected what was theirs, period.

"Yeah, I do." The sheriff shook Alan's hand and then did the same to Sawyer. "I will keep my eyes open, and you all be safe. Don't go off on your own. Stay in touch with each other. None of this deciding to go out sleeping under the damned stars for a few days." He opened the door to his cruiser and climbed inside. "And for God's sake, don't do anything stupid." He closed the door and pulled out of the drive.

"Okay," Sawyer said. "I guess he had to have the last word." He half expected Alan to get angry with him. It was his fault that his father had come to find him and brought all this potential danger to the ranch. Maybe he really should leave. At least the people here on the ranch, the ones he cared about, would be safe.

"Just stop," Alan told him sharply. "I know what you're thinking, because it's the same crap I'd be thinking. You didn't do this, and it isn't your fault. Your father is the one who gambled and racked up the debts." Alan lifted his hat and scratched his head. "Maybe we need to talk to Claude's friend. We need someone in that world who can tell us what's going on."

"I can't afford to bring in security experts."

Alan growled. "Don't even go there." He turned and headed to the house. Sawyer stayed where he was, wondering how fast he could pack his shit. "Come on. Don't just stand there." He held the door, and Sawyer sighed and went inside.

Mrs. J had gone to bed, but the others were still hanging around the living room. Claude joined them with a glass of whiskey, offering the others some as well. Randall accepted a glass, and Sawyer did as well because he needed it to calm his jangled nerves. "I called my friend in Dallas, and he's sending someone. They'll be here in the morning."

"Do we really need to do that?" Sawyer asked.

Claude clapped him on the shoulder. "Yeah, we do. I don't know anything about gambling debt collection, and Jase, one of the guys in my friend's firm, knows all about it. He worked in casinos in Louisiana and Mississippi."

Sawyer sipped the whiskey, the warmth sliding down his throat. "If you think this is for the best. I just don't want you all to go through all this effort because of me."

"It's because of your father, not you," Randall said quietly from next to him. "This isn't your fault." He lightly bumped his shoulder, and Sawyer wondered what he'd have done if Randall hadn't been here. His first impressions about him had been wrong, and Sawyer was pleased that he was here. No one had backed him up the way Randall had, and the man barely knew him. One thing was clear: Randall had a good heart, and that was what mattered. He closed his eyes as Randall's scent threatened to overwhelm him. Yeah, the guy was hot, and those eyes of his sometimes made him forget his name.

But… none of that really mattered. He couldn't get involved with him. The idea that sophisticated Randall could be interested in a rough cowboy like him was ridiculous. George and Alan worked, but lightning like that was not going to strike twice—and definitely not for him.

Chapter 7

THE HOUSE was quiet, and Randall had the window open for some fresh air, otherwise it would be stifling. The wind rushed outside, insects sang, and cattle made their soft sounds. A few days ago it would have been unsettling, but not tonight. He knew what the sounds were now, and they were comforting. What he didn't expect was a creak on the floor outside his room. Randall listened for the sound again and quietly got up, slipping out of his room and down the hall. Not that he expected that someone had broken in, but his mind refused to turn off.

"What are you doing up?" Sawyer asked as he stood at the sink in the kitchen with a glass. Randall swallowed hard, his throat dry. Sawyer wore a pair of shorts and nothing else, his skin tanned and golden in the light from above the stove. Damn, his imagination had filled in some of the detail when he closed his eyes, but he really needed to work on it—he had definitely come up short.

"I was going to ask you the same thing," Randall said. He got a glass himself and opened the refrigerator for some juice. He was about to sit down when Sawyer went to the living room and sat near the front window. "Is this what you do when you can't sleep?"

Sawyer shrugged. "Sometimes, I guess. I don't know. Usually I work hard enough that by the end of the day, I fall into bed and just sleep. Then I get up and do it all over again. I guess that's the product of an honest, hardworking life." He sighed and turned to look outside again. "At least that's what I thought I was doing. I don't know now."

"Your father isn't you, and he isn't a reflection of you," Randall said. "Look, my father was a drunk most of the time. He called it social drinking, but it was too much by whatever name he wanted to give it, and it rotted his brain. So I know what addiction and compulsion can do to someone. I also know what they do to their family." He sat in the chair next to Sawyer. "And this has nothing to do with you. I can promise you that." A flash came from outside, and Randall leaned closer, watching as it came again.

"There's a storm," he said quietly. "I hope it makes its way over here. We could use the rain."

"I hate storms," Randall whispered. "I used to lie in my bed with my eyes closed and tremble. My parents were usually in bed, and I was never allowed to go in their room. And my nannies… they wouldn't stand for it. So I suffered through it alone." He turned back to Sawyer, unable to look away from him.

"Do you have any brothers or sisters?" Sawyer asked. "I was an only child."

"I had an older brother and a younger sister. My older brother died before he was a year old. He was born with a heart condition, and there was little they could do for him. That was so hard on my mom, at least that's what she told me. Then she had me, and I was healthy, and she always said she was happy. Then she and my father had Rachel. She was their favorite, I know that, and they doted on her. But when she was five, she was at a friend's playing and the kids went outside. Rachel apparently ran into the street to get the ball and she was hit by a car." He remembered all of that, every miserable moment. Including the funeral, and then the way the grief seemed to tear his mom and dad apart. "It was never the same." That was the understatement of the century.

More flashes lit the night, getting brighter, the rumbles of thunder louder. Randall pulled out his phone and brought up a radar app, then showed the approaching area of green and yellow to Sawyer. He turned away from the window. "What are you doing?" Sawyer asked when Randall's gaze stopped on him. It refused to move.

"Watching you," he answered honestly before he could think of some sort of cover.

"Oh," Sawyer said as a roll of thunder rumbled through the house. Then he jumped up and hurried back toward his room. He returned a few minutes later with a shirt on and boots. "We need to get the horses inside." Sawyer hurried out the door as Randall returned to his room, where he pulled on his boots and a pair of his new jeans before following him outside.

The wind whipped as he crossed the yard, moisture filling the air. He hurried into the barn and opened one of the paddock doors. The horse came right inside and into the stalls. Randall closed the sliding door and latched it before heading to the next one. He whistled when the horse wasn't waiting to be let in, and she trotted over and into the stall, heading right for the hay. He did the rest for all the stalls on that side the barn before coming to the final stall. When he opened it, the horse shied away, racing to the far side of the paddock.

Thunder cracked, and he reared. Randall stepped out, speaking softly, letting the wind carry his voice. "It's okay. Just relax. I'm going to get you inside where it's dry and you can eat all the hay you want." He drew closer, the horse listening and staying on four legs.

"Randall," Sawyer said from behind him as he reached the harness, taking it and patting his neck.

"It's okay," he said gently, leading the horse to the barn, hoping to all hell that another clap of thunder didn't spook him again. As soon as he got close enough to see the hay and the stall, he took off inside just as lightning lit up the night and thunder split the air. The horse bucked, and Sawyer hurried outside and closed the door behind him, leaving both of them in the paddock as the sky opened up.

They were drenched in seconds. "Are they all inside?" Randall asked.

"Yes." Sawyer hurried toward the front, and they climbed the fences until they reached the front of the barn. Sawyer pulled the door closed and then they ran to the house, stopping in the mudroom.

"Everything okay?" Alan asked once they had closed the door.

"Yeah," Sawyer answered, pulling off his boots and turning them upside down to drain out the water. Randall's jeans clung to him, but he got his boots off and stood dripping on the tiled mudroom floor. "Everything is fine. Randall here even got Hurricane in the barn."

"How?" Alan asked. "That horse freaks out at every storm." He smiled. "Good job. That's no small feat." He yawned and tossed towels at both of them. "I'm going back to bed. Turn out the lights behind you." He yawned again and his footsteps retreated.

"I need to get out of these jeans," Randall groaned. "But I think they shrank on me." He tried to get them down, but the damned things didn't want to budge.

"Unbutton the pants and jump up on the washer," Sawyer told him. Randall did as he asked, and Sawyer tugged at the bottom of the legs. The jeans began to slide, and once he raised his hips, they slid off his legs. Sawyer dropped them into the wash tub with a splat. Randall couldn't help laughing.

"I don't know if I'm ever going to get those on again."

"It'll be fine. We can wash them in the morning and stretch them a little. For now, we should get out of the rest of these wet clothes and go back to bed. It looks like it's going to rain for a while, and in the morning, we'll have to clean up whatever the wind decided to blow around."

"Will it be bad?"

"Probably not, but you never know," Sawyer said, and Randall followed him down the hall and to their rooms. He went inside and got out of his wet shirt, then pulled out something dry to sleep in before quietly sneaking across the hall to the bathroom to hang up the wet things. When he opened the door, he found Sawyer outside, and it seemed it was his turn to stare.

"Sorry," he whispered, and Randall scurried around him and headed to his room. He made it to the door before a hand rested on his shoulder. Randall turned, staring into huge, surprised eyes.

"Yeah?" he asked, ready to go back to bed. In an instant, Randall remembered what his back looked like and why those marks were there. "Look, I...."

"Who the hell did that to you?" Sawyer asked. His voice was soft but vehement, his eyes blazing with suppressed fury. He touched Randall's back, and Randall flinched for a second, but Sawyer was gentle, his fingers warm and only a little rough. "What kind of person would beat you like this?" He drew closer, and Randall felt the heat washing off him. He didn't dare turn around, even though tingles radiated from each point of contact.

"My father," Randall finally answered. "I told you he drank too much, and when he did and I did something he didn't like...." His voice ached with the old pain. "He used to have a razor strop, and he'd wield it like a whip when he was drunk and angry, which was most of the time. He never controlled himself very well, so even today, when someone has too much to drink, I avoid them. I got really good at being away from my father when I was on school breaks. I had a hideout in the stables that he didn't know about, and I even had one in the attic of the estate and one in the kitchens. My father rarely went down there. He might have lost his temper, but he always did it when we were alone. The staff had no idea. Well, most of them didn't."

Sawyer placed his hand on his right shoulder blade. "Your father really did this to you? And I thought mine was a jackass and a half, but this takes the cake. How could anyone do this to someone else?" He drew closer, his hands gliding over his skin and along the lines Randall's father had carved into his hide. "It's just mean. Did your mother know?"

"She was already dead before he started acting this way. I know my father loved her. Hell, she was probably the only person in the world he truly cared for other than himself, and after she died, he went off the deep end. That's when the bad drinking started and he…." Randall had said more than enough. This was too painful to hash over, and his father was dead. There was no use dredging up what was best left in the past.

A gentle kiss ghosted over his skin.

"What was that for?" Randall asked.

"My mama used to kiss my knees whenever I skinned them. She said it would make them feel better." He did it again, and Randall slowly turned around. "And it seems a shame that no one tried to make you feel better. There should have been someone to stand up for you."

"Not against him. He was the earl, so everyone deferred to him. He was very used to it and liked it. Damned idiocy made him feel important and smart. But he was dumb as a stump, I swear. The man could barely add, and he never read anything other than the label on a whiskey bottle. But he thought everyone in the village should come by and ask his advice before they did anything. And when they stopped because his advice was usually wrong, it only deepened his sink into the bottle." He didn't dare move, not wanting the break the connection with Sawyer's deep blue eyes.

"You don't want to talk about this anymore, do you?" Sawyer prompted. More than anything, Randall wanted to forget that part of his life, but he bore constant reminders of it on his body. He shook his head slowly. "The scars…."

"I know they're ugly. I've been told that by almost everyone who saw them. I used to stay out of the locker rooms until everyone else had left so I could change without others seeing."

Sawyer drew closer. "Bullshit. They're scars. We all have them. Some on the outside where they can be seen, and some on the inside. Those are the ones that are worse, because no one knows they're there but us." Sawyer gently turned him around, then ran his fingers over the scarred skin, sending ripples racing through him that Randall didn't quite know how to parse. Were they desire or weirdness? Maybe a combination of both.

"But…." He was supposed to be strong and a leader. That was the role he was born into, and the one his father had failed at. He wasn't supposed to feel this way about his own body.

"These are war wounds." Sawyer rested his hand flat on his shoulder blade. "They happened because of what someone else did to you. And you survived and were strong enough to heal and go on. Your father is dead and he can't hurt you any longer, so really, you came out the winner." Sawyer pulled away, and Randall had to see into his eyes to know if he was serious or just humoring him. When he turned and looked into them again, he saw heat and desire reflected back at him.

This was a bad idea, but it was just the two of them standing in the damned hallway outside his room. Randall slipped into it, not looking away from Sawyer, who seemed to follow him, drawn by an invisible string. Neither of them moved nearer to the other until Sawyer shut the door. Then he closed the distance, drawing Randall into his strong cowboy arms and moving to kiss him. "Is this okay?" Sawyer's voice was rough and deep.

Randall nodded, and Sawyer bridged the last gap between them, sealing their lips together in a kiss that made Randall's head spin. He had been with a number of guys. Hell, Randall was no shrinking violet, but Sawyer seemed so forceful and sure that Randall found himself taking a back seat, letting Sawyer lead the way.

Sawyer pressed him back toward the bed until the backs of Randall's legs hit the mattress. Sawyer paused, sliding his hands down Randall's back and into his sleep shorts, then slipping them down his ass and legs until his cock popped free. Randall sighed as the fabric slid down his legs, and he stepped out of them. He was bare in front of Sawyer, and almost instantly, his very own cowboy was just as naked. And damn… now he understood why the guys had come here, because cowboys were bloody hot.

"Hey, you gonna keep looking or what?" Sawyer stepped back and slowly turned around.

"What are you doing?"

"Giving you a gander at the full package." He came to a stop after doing his cowboy pirouette. "You seen enough?"

"I don't know if that will ever be possible," Randall said as he pulled Sawyer to him. Their kisses grew in intensity. Sawyer pressed him further, and before Randall knew it, he was falling back onto the bed, bouncing slightly.

Sawyer leaned over him, growing closer. Randall wound his arms around his neck to reel him in. "Do you think this is a good idea?"

Sawyer groaned. "Sometimes you think way too much." He kissed him, and Randall had to agree—sometimes thought was way overrated… and this was definitely one of those times. He was naked and in bed with the sexiest man he had ever met, one he really liked, and all he could wonder about was if this was a good idea. Of course it was—it was fantastic. He let himself sink into the moment, with Sawyer caressing his chest, that amazing touch sliding downward. He held his breath as Sawyer stroked his hip, and then he moaned softly into their kiss as his touch settled on his belly.

Sawyer seemed intent on going slowly, while Randall was as hyped up as he could remember being. "How can you be so calm? I want you more than I have ever wanted anyone." He felt like he was sputtering.

Sawyer pulled back. "I want you too, and that's why we need to go slow."

"That doesn't make sense."

Sawyer smiled. "Sure it does. It means that you and I only get one first time together, and I intend to make sure that it's the most mind-blowing sex you have ever had so you'll remember it long after you have to go home." He stopped Randall from saying anything more by kissing him again, and this time, Randall stopped talking. They had all night. And hell, whatever Sawyer had in mind for the two of them was more than fine with him. The way he felt at this moment, Randall could stay like this for hours.

The light through the window hit his eyes, and Randall groggily came to. He tried to remember if what happened last night was real or a dream. Then he rolled over and bumped into Sawyer, who startled awake, sitting right up, the sheets pooling around his waist. "I need to get to work." He jumped out of bed and hurried around, pulling on the few clothes he'd been wearing before they'd attacked each other.

"Okay. I guess…."

Sawyer leaned over the bed. "It's just that I have chores. It's not like I'm running out on you. This ranch ain't that big." Then he kissed him. "Work first, and tonight you and me can have as much fun as we can stand." He kissed him again before quietly leaving the room. Randall stayed in bed for a few seconds before pushing back the covers and searching in his bag. He got dressed and hurried out to the barn, where Sawyer was already checking the horses and letting them out in the paddocks after the storm.

"Was there any damage?" Randall asked.

"Not that I can tell, and it's too nice a day for them to stay in here." He opened the doors, and the horses ambled out into the sunshine.

"You're not supposed to be alone, remember?"

"I'm just in the barn," Sawyer said as though it wasn't a big deal. "There are plenty of folks here. I don't think anyone is going to try anything here on the property." He finished with the horses and slid the door closed. "What has you so wound up?"

"These collection people are not going to respect the ranch boundaries. If they think they can get you to pay, they will come anywhere and do just about anything. These aren't lawyers. They're bounty hunters, and they sure as hell don't care about things like that. So you need to stay around others and keep your eyes open."

Sawyer grabbed the shovel and leaned on it slightly. "You really think they are going to come after a broke cowboy like me? I don't have any money to pay them. I don't own anything but my truck, and you can tell they ain't getting much for that."

"Maybe not, but how do you think Mrs. J or Alan are going to feel if you get grabbed? They might pay, or maybe they shoot you and then threaten them?" Randall drew closer. "Just be careful and don't take any chances. That's all I'm saying."

"Okay. Maybe you know best. Now, I have to get this finished, and you can help." He handed Randall the shovel. "The horses were in the stalls all night, so give them a spot clean, and then we can set about looking over the colts. I want to see how they're settling in and maybe work with them a little. Get a halter on them and maybe see how they respond to a lead. Not too much, but we can assess their behavior."

"Okay. You're the boss." He grabbed the shovel and a wheelbarrow and got started. "Do you have any idea how tickled all the people in the village would be to see me mucking out stalls?"

"They'd probably like you all the more for it." Sawyer strode away before pausing and then pulling out his phone to snap a picture.

"What was that for?"

"To keep you humble." He grinned as he left the barn. Randall groaned and rolled his eyes before getting to work.

Chapter 8

"Sawyer," Mrs. J called, standing near the paddock as he let the colt run on the lead. Hercules, Zeus, and Poseidon had all taken to the halter and lead pretty easily. "How did they do?"

"Exceedingly well," Sawyer said, slowing the colt to a walk. Then he came to a stop, approaching Sawyer to nuzzle his chest. "They are all very good, and they seem eager to please. All three of them were raised well. They aren't skittish in the least. I think when we're ready to train them, they'll respond well." He patted the colt's neck before leading him to his home paddock and removing the lead. He joined the others, the three of them frolicking like they hadn't seen each other in a while.

"You have a real good eye," Sawyer told her. "Especially for auction horses."

"Well, I knew the owner and his reputation." She tapped the fence nervously. "They came from the Molton place. Heather always knew how to breed amazing horses. She had the knack, and these are her last three." She eyed the colts as they settled in to eat.

"I heard she passed away about six months ago." Heather Molton was legendary in their part of the country.

"She did. And since she didn't have any family, she left it all to charity, and they were selling off everything. I was able to get these three horses at the auction. I would have bought every one they had, but I could only afford these." She swallowed. "She and I went to school together." She raised her gaze as Randall came over to join them, his boots and pant legs filthy.

"Were you friends?" Sawyer asked.

"More like frenemies, I guess. We knew each other, but we were also rivals in a lot of ways. She was always smart and driven. I was popular, and we butted heads a lot growing up, but as we got older, we came to respect each other and realized that we could support each other instead of competing. I like to think she'd be happy that these boys are here and will be given a good home."

"So you aren't raising them to sell?" Sawyer asked.

Mrs. J sighed. "I'm not sure. See, the one unknown with these guys is what she was breeding them to do. Heather was secretive about her plans and methodologies. Her colts and fillies went on to become amazing cutting and riding horses. Others are champions of dressage, and a few are racing out east. She had this ability to breed some interesting animals. She always believed that a horse would show what its abilities were in its own time. So that's what we're going to do here. I want to find out what these boys are good at. Let their abilities come forward."

"There aren't a lot of racehorses here in Wyoming," Sawyer said.

"I don't know about that. They may not be trained here, but racehorses and steeplechasers can come from nowhere," Randall said. "Think of Seabiscuit and any number of other horses. Sometimes you never know."

"Did you ever keep racehorses?" Mrs. J asked.

Randall shook his head and explained what had happened to his family's stables. Sawyer had already heard the story, so he half tuned it out and watched Randall. There was deep regret in his stance, and Sawyer wanted to bring the old earl back from the dead so he could kill him all over again.

A slick car, very low to the ground, slowly turned into the drive. "We don't get many of those around here," Mrs. J said as they all watched the powder-blue Porsche maneuver down the drive before parking near the house.

Sawyer glanced at Randall, who shrugged as a man got out of the car. He was relatively small but very well dressed. Sawyer thought at first that he was here to see Randall. He imagined that guys like this with fancy cars and three-thousand-dollar suits would be part of his world, but the man spoke briefly with Mrs. J, and then she looked over at Sawyer.

"What can I do for you?" Sawyer asked as he approached.

"Sawyer Kincaid?" He held out his hand, and Sawyer took it. "I'm Jase Easton. I understand you're having some trouble with bill collectors of a certain ilk."

"Well, not exactly." Sawyer began, and Randall cleared his throat. "Yeah, sorry. I'm forgetting my manners. This is Randall; he's staying with us." He wasn't sure if he should explain that he was an earl but figured if Randall wanted him to know, then he could explain.

Jase nodded. "I wish we were meeting under better circumstances." He returned to his car and retrieved a leather case. "Shall we?"

"Of course. Sawyer, you can use the living room to talk over what you need to." She patted him on the shoulder and then went inside.

"I don't really know how much I can tell you," Sawyer said as he led the way through, taking off his boots in the mud room. He wasn't going to disrespect Mrs. J by tracking dirt into her house.

Randall took off his boots as well, and they all traipsed into the living room. Sawyer and Randall sat on the sofa, and Jase sat across from them in one of the chairs. The man was probably comfortable in just about any surroundings. "Why don't you tell me what's going on?"

"Well, I don't know much. A lot of this is supposition. My father has a gambling problem, and he came to me for money, which means he's desperate. Badly so. So I figure he's in over his head and owes someone big-time."

Jase nodded.

"I have some experience with things like this, and I didn't want Sawyer to be caught up in his father's mess," Randall said.

"Well, you were smart. Last night when I was given this case, I did some research with a few contacts I have, and it seems that Howard Kincaid has racked up some serious debts to a number of casinos. I'm afraid it isn't just one. He owes money in Louisiana and Alabama. It seems he was playing in one place hoping to pay off his debts to another, and now no one will let him play and they are coming to collect." He opened his case and pulled out some paperwork. "These are people who play hardball."

Sawyer swallowed hard, because shit and damn. What was he supposed to do? "I'm just a cowboy, and I don't have a lot of money. And even if I did, I'm not paying for his debts. That isn't fair."

"The law is on your side. He's responsible for this, not you. But I'm here because these people don't play by the law—at least when people owe them money and they think they can get away with it."

"Do you have any idea how far they are behind him?" Randall asked.

Jase chuckled. "The wolves are nipping at his heels. My guess is that they found him a few days ago and that's why he came to you. I take it you and your father are not on good terms." He was all business. The guy looked more like a lawyer than a security specialist.

"No. My father was abusive and a total piece of shit. I don't care why he was coming to me. I did my best to get him out of my life, and I want it to stay that way."

"Okay, then." He closed his case. "These collectors will try to intimidate you and anyone they think is close enough to your father or you to try to get them to pay up. It's what they do. Now the good thing is that they just want to be paid and then they go away. But…."

"I don't have enough money to pay them." Frustration grew in his voice.

"I get that. And once they exhaust their options with your father, they will try to intimidate you. Has anyone approached you?"

Sawyer shook his head. Maybe these people would leave him alone.

Alan came in with George right behind him. Sawyer hated that he had brought all this trouble here. This was something none of these folks should have to deal with.

"This is Alan and his husband, George," Sawyer explained.

Jase nodded and they sat down.

Alan spoke first. "What do we need to do to keep Sawyer and everyone here safe? My men all have guns, and they know how to use them. If these people trespass, we can take them out." Damn, Alan was as wound up and serious as Sawyer had ever seen him.

"The biggest thing you can do is show these guys you're strong when they show up. Make sure they know that trying to come after you is going to be a hell of a lot of trouble."

"Is that all the advice that you have?" Alan asked. "These people have no right to come here or demand anything. We have made the sheriff aware of the possibility of trouble, and he's going to be on the lookout. This is a small town, and I somehow doubt that they are going to receive any support or cover from anyone here."

"That's better than I had expected."

"The sheriff will give them my father if he gets the chance, but that's between the two of them." Sawyer swallowed as another notion occurred to him. "Do you think my father will just 'disappear' and never be seen again?"

Jase shrugged. "I don't know. I was asked to come here and give you an honest assessment of the situation."

Footsteps hurried in from the kitchen, and everyone turned. Chip almost skidded to a halt, his eyes huge. "What's this? Did I miss a family meeting or something?" He looked at everyone in turn. "Is this about Sawyer's dad? I saw him in town this morning." His eyes grew wider. "He had a black eye and was walking funny. I think someone beat him up pretty bad."

"They know where he is, and they've most likely given him a deadline."

Sawyer groaned. "Which means he's going to get more and more desperate." Great, just what he needed. More trouble. "And it means we can expect to see him pretty soon. When it comes to saving his own skin, he isn't going to stop trying to get to me."

"You have plenty of people behind you," Randall said quietly.

"Yes, you do," Alan told him. "What can you do to help?" he added to Jase.

"I was asked to provide an assessment, and if I'm honest, I could bring in a number of people to beef up security and turn the ranch into a fortress. It's all a matter of the resources that you want to put into it. But that may be massive overkill. I'd like to stay for a few days if you're agreeable and keep an eye on things. I'd also like to see if I can find out who they are. So far we've talked about them as nameless, faceless people. Once we know who we're looking for, we might be able to see them coming. It would be stupid of them to cause enough trouble that they bring extra attention to themselves."

"They were foolish enough to let my father bet on credit, so they aren't the brightest bulbs on the string."

"See what you can dig up. If we're going to have to fight, then we need to know who we're taking on. From there we can devise a plan to keep everyone safe. Because damn it all, this is really starting to piss me off," Alan said.

"Me too," Randall whispered from next to him before he placed his hand on Sawyer's.

"Do you really think I should just sit here and do nothing?" Sawyer asked once everyone had left the meeting. Jase had said that he was going to try to perform some additional research.

"I know this: there is strength in numbers. So let Jase do his job, and we'll do ours, which is making sure that everyone on this ranch is safe," Alan told him, holding his gaze until Sawyer nodded. "Good man." Then he exited the room, leaving Sawyer and Randall alone.

"I feel so helpless." And that went against everything in his nature. He liked being in control of his life, and this was the exact opposite. Without thinking, he leaned against Randall.

"Sometimes we all need help," Randall said softly. "You know I hate talking about this, but after my dad would beat me for whatever he thought I had done, I used to hide in my room for days because I didn't want anyone to know. I'd take food from the kitchen and eat in there just so no one would see me. Once I could cover the hurt, then I'd come out and act like everything was normal. I was so ashamed of what had happened, like his actions were my fault."

Sawyer nodded slowly. "Yeah, I get that."

"This is not your fault any more than I was responsible for what my deranged father did. He was sick in a lot of ways. But I let him make me feel guilty. You can't do that. The only way to stop it is to stand up to him."

"Did you ever do that?"

Randall nodded. "I did. Just before he died. He was drunk and angry. He came after me with the strap, but this time I grabbed it from him. I yanked it away and refused to give it back, and when he came at me this final time, I swung it low and got him in the legs. He went down, yowling like an idiot. I swung at him once more, getting him across the back. My father hit the floor and passed out. I don't even think he remembered what happened when he came to. But the strap was gone. I burned it, and then I went back to school. I never saw him again, and just after I turned eighteen, he died and I inherited the estate, the title, and the responsibilities that he had largely been shirking for years."

"Yeah, I get it. I really do." He rested his head on Randall's shoulder. "Some people were never meant to be parents. People have to be approved to adopt a dog from a shelter, but anyone can have a kid."

"Yeah. Well… I guess all we can do is our best with the situation we're given."

"Yeah. We take it one day at a time."

"And hope we don't screw it up," Randall said flatly. "And if we're done trying to out-cliché each other now?"

Sawyer chuckled softly. "Okay. You got me on that one. Now, we have work to do, and it isn't going to do itself."

"I was hoping that since we got the stalls cleaned already and that with all the excitement of the last few days… maybe we could go for a ride? I haven't had a chance to see anything of Wyoming other than the ranch."

Alan returned, standing in the doorway.

"I can't just leave," Sawyer said.

"Actually, you can," Alan interrupted. "Go away for a few days. Take one of the ranch vehicles and see some sights. Randall can go with you if he wants. If your father shows up, we can say that we don't know where you are and that he should get the hell out of Dodge. Things here aren't going to fall apart over a couple of days."

"Are you sure?" Sawyer asked. It seemed like a lot.

"Go. Let us see if a little absence can help defuse this situation." He waved, and Sawyer went down to the room he was using. He grabbed his bag and hurried out to the bunkhouse, where he packed enough for a couple of days before meeting Randall in the yard. They tossed their things behind the seat in the truck and took off out of the ranch drive.

"Where to?" Randall asked.

"We're a couple hours from Grand Teton. We could go there. It's beautiful, with the peaks and the river valleys. Yellowstone is probably farther than we should travel for a few days." Though it was one of his favorite places. He had vacationed there a number of times, but the distance was a little too much.

"Will I get to see geysers?" Randall asked.

"No. Those are only in Yellowstone. But there are plenty of other things to see. I hope that's okay."

Randall smiled. "I'm sure it will be great."

Sawyer drove to the highway going north, and they settled in. "Is everywhere here like this?" Randall asked as they drove toward the mountain range. "I mean, there are peaks all around. England has hills, but nothing like this."

"Yeah. Welcome to the northern Rockies. Can you imagine being one of those first settlers heading west? They crossed pass after pass thinking the next one was the last. But the mountains went on for five hundred miles in some places. Now we drive through them easily, but not back then when all they had were horses, oxen, mules, and a wagon."

Randall continued looking out the windows, his head going from side to side. "How long does it take to get from one side of the state to the other?"

"It's about three hundred and fifty miles from one side to the other, but some parts of the state are pretty remote. There isn't a lot of population here in Wyoming, and a lot of the state is owned by the federal government, so there are huge unspoiled and wild spaces. Over the years, that led to a lot of tension, but today we have some amazing resources that would have otherwise been lost." Sawyer continued driving as Randall practically pressed his nose to the glass like one of Chip's dogs. Even Sawyer had to admit that the scenery was pretty amazing, but what kept turning his head was the sight sitting in the passenger seat. Sawyer knew that his heart had woken up and that he was developing strong feelings for Randall, ones he should put out the way he'd stomp a burning ember into the ground. After all, he would return to his fancy life as lord of the manor soon. Sawyer knew he'd also be back on his own again, and he might as well get used to it.

He pushed that notion away. What the fuck was he doing? He shook his head.

"What are you thinking about?" Randall asked.

"Nothing," Sawyer answered quickly with a smile. He needed to get that notion out of his head. Randall had been here barely a week, and while he liked the guy, he was not going to fall in love with him in that short period of time. And even if that was happening… he was happy. Damn it all, he was enjoying the time with Randall, and if that came with disappointment at the end, so be it. He would take what he could get for as long as it lasted and deal with the crap at the other end when it arrived. Hell, he dealt with horses every single day, and he knew what to do with the crap that always seemed to flow no matter what. Shovel it, dump it on the muck pile, and move on. And that was what he'd do now.

"Are you woolgathering?" Randall asked.

"I don't know what that means," Sawyer said, pulling himself back into the moment. He reached over and took Randall's hand, determined to stay in the here and now for as long as it lasted.

CHAPTER 9

RANDALL COULD barely breathe as they came to a stop at the scenic overlook. They had been driving for about three hours, and suddenly he found it impossible to look away. Randall opened the truck door, mesmerized by the sight in front of him. This view was famous, with so many pictures published of it that he might have thought it redundant, but seeing the place in person made him realize how flat all the images seemed.

"The mountains look like you can reach out and touch them." Randall used the same voice he had when he was a child and his parents had dragged him to church. He knew he was in some grand space that might belong to God.

"The mountains themselves are miles away, but they seem right there." Sawyer reached out with a smile.

The valley below them seemed lush, with rivers and even a lake. It was hard to tell how large they were because everything seemed small as the line of jagged peaks rose above them. Randall shifted closer to Sawyer, unable to look away. Sawyer slipped an arm around him, and they stood, just the two of them, in the late afternoon light as the shadows of the peaks slowly spread over the valley, while the peaks themselves seemed to blaze as the snow still clinging to the tops glowed and sparkled. "The Grand Tetons."

"Yeah. This is them. They're also called the Sisters and goodness knows what else."

"Teton comes from the French," Randall said and leaned closer. "It means teats."

Sawyer groaned. "I was told as a kid that the name refers to one of the Western Sioux tribes, and I think that's a lot better. When I was a kid, I helped out on a dairy farm, and believe me, I saw more than my share of teats. So let's leave it at the tribe." He sighed.

"What's that for?"

"Just thinking. That's all."

"About what?" Randall asked. "I believe that a place like this is the perfect location to think. My parents went to church and all that. I don't really, not anymore, given the church's stance on people like us. I'm not really sure what I believe, but this place makes you think that a god is possible and that he might choose to stay extra close. I would, just for the view." He didn't want to blink in case he missed something.

Sawyer leaned closer. "That was pretty." He grew quiet, and Randall figured he deserved the privacy of his thoughts. Whatever they were, they could stay between him and the god that Randall seemed to sense. Maybe it was stupid, but he was content in the moment, the two of them alone. He turned, and Sawyer did the same. Without thinking, he tugged Sawyer to him, kissing him hard, letting the awe and majesty of the location flow between them. Because Sawyer made him feel the exact same way. Sawyer filled him with a sense of something bigger than himself. But he couldn't label what it was. Every time he tried, the words slipped away, but the feeling remained.

An approaching car broke the moment, and they pulled away, staring at each other as tires crunched on the gravel. A family piled out, with kids talking excitedly and parents standing together to watch the mountain, the same way they had. "Come on. There's plenty more to see."

Randall nodded, and they got back in the truck and pulled out of the overlook and back onto the road. The view shifted slightly as they rode with the sun growing lower in the sky. "Where are we going?"

"Don't worry. I have everything all set," Sawyer told him, and he sat back and watched the scenery as the sun reached the top of the peaks and then dipped behind them, their shadows finally catching up with them. Sawyer took his hand, and they rode in silence as the last of the light faded behind the peaks.

"WHERE ARE we going?" Randall asked again as they bumped along a road just off the highway. They passed a sign that the lights illuminated, but he didn't have a chance to read it before the darkness enveloped it once more.

"To our lodgings for the night," Sawyer said and then slowed and nearly pulled to a stop before making a final turn. The truck lights shone on a small cabin.

"Is that it?" Randall asked. He was starting to wonder if Sawyer had taken it upon himself to try to give him the true frontier experience.

"Yes." He pulled out his phone and, after a few seconds, grinned and got out of the truck. Sawyer grabbed their bags and headed toward the cabin. At the door, he reached for the lock box thing and put in a code. Then he went inside and turned on the lights.

Randall hadn't known what to expect, and the place wasn't palatial, but it was rustic and comfortable, the furniture simple but nice. There was a single room with a bed and a few chairs, and a kitchenette along the one wall.

"How did you find this?" Randall asked as he sat on the side of the bed. It was comfortable, and the bedding was thick and soft.

"One of the guys from town stayed here, and he told me about it. I called when we stopped to use the bathroom this afternoon. It seemed like a good idea."

"Did you use a credit card?" Randall asked. "Because they can trace it."

Sawyer drew closer. "The owner of the cabin lives in Cheyenne, and he has a business, so if they trace it, they'll end up in the wrong place. So it's not a big deal." He sat next to him. "Everything is going to be okay. They're going to take their pound of flesh out of my father."

"But we're in the middle of nowhere," Randall said. The place really seemed remote, and it was even quieter than the ranch, which he didn't think possible. Sawyer opened the windows, and the sounds of the night seemed to assault him. It wasn't as quiet as he thought, just a different kind of sounds. No cars or people noises—just nature.

"That's the beauty of it. There are other cabins. They're about fifty yards apart, so there are people around, just not close."

"I see," Randall said. "So it's just you and me."

"Yeah. Are you hungry? A few things came stocked with the cabin." Instead of answering, Randall kissed him, and the cool night air coming through the window did nothing to chill the heat that built between them. He held Sawyer tightly, their kisses becoming more intense by the second. All he wanted was to feast on Sawyer and have him all to himself. There was no one that could hear them, and there were no chores to get up for. Randall could have Sawyer all night long, and he was determined to take advantage.

RANDALL WOKE as light came through the windows. His was totally relaxed and kind of sex hungover. Sawyer had spread out in the night, an arm under his head, the covers pooled around his waist. If Randall had any artistic talent, he would have wanted to paint the image of his cowboy still asleep, as beautiful and sexy as anything he had ever seen. Randall had traveled through Europe and been to all the great museums, and yet Sawyer, his cowboy, was more beautiful than anything he had ever seen. Randall didn't want to move. He didn't want Sawyer to stir and change the moment. And yet just waking up and wishing it wouldn't change had done just that.

"What are you doin'?" Sawyer asked as he slid open his deep blue eyes.

"Watching," Randall said, barely breathing. "I'm just looking at you." Everything outside was still. The birds hadn't started singing yet. It was like everything was just waking up, taking the first deep breath before getting started. Then a single bird called from outside the window, and the rest joined in, beginning the first notes of the symphony of sound that would last until the sun set.

"Settle back down," Sawyer told him with a wide yawn. "We ain't at the ranch, and we don't need to get up with the sun. Not today." He gathered Randall in his arms, tugging him close before kissing him. Randall thought that might have been the start of their morning, but Sawyer closed his eyes once more, just holding him, and soon Randall drifted back to sleep.

WHEN HE woke again, it was to Sawyer stroking his chest, lips at the base of his neck. "I knew I could get your attention," Sawyer whispered before returning to his particularly amazing wake-up call.

"Sawyer," Randall whispered, stretching his neck, his entire body waking up. He wound his fingers through Sawyer's soft hair and closed his eyes, immersing his senses in the sensation of Sawyer's lips on him. "God…."

Sawyer backed away for a split second before taking his lips in a bruising kiss. Randall wound his arms around Sawyer's neck, pressing the two of them together. Their bodies melded easily, sending waves of excitement through him. Sawyer's muscles rippled under his touch, and each time he inhaled, Sawyer's scent built, becoming stronger and amazingly more powerful with each breath, like it was carrying Randall away… and he willingly went right along with it.

"I want all of you," Sawyer whispered. "And I don't know how to do that." He pulled away. "I want to feel you and see all of you. It's like I can't get enough, and every time I try, part of you slips away and I have to chase it."

"Is that bad?" Randall asked, trying to understand.

"Hell no. I love a good chase," Sawyer told him.

Randall chuckled, looking into Sawyer's eyes. "Then I guess I'll have to think of other ways to keep you on your toes."

"You do that," Sawyer nearly growled. "That's enough talk," he declared, and kissed him again, building up the heat between them until Randall shook with energy he didn't know what to do with. "Did you bring… stuff?" Randall stilled and then shook his head. They'd left fast enough that he hadn't thought about that. "No problem…."

"Okay," Randall whispered as Sawyer shucked off the covers and slid down him before taking Randall between his lips. The wet heat was sublime, and he groaned softly, becoming louder and more insistent as Sawyer took him harder, sucking more vigorously, bobbing his head, tugging on him with his lips until Randall knew he was going to come unglued at any second. He gripped the bedding, using it to anchor himself in the present or else he was going to fly apart. "What are you doing to me?" Randall whispered.

"Tasting you?" Sawyer answered before taking him once more, and this time Randall barely had a chance to breathe before he was flying. For a second he imagined himself over those grand peaks, seeing them from the air like a bird. Then Sawyer drove him higher and the peaks got smaller; he flew faster until he could contain it no more. Clamping his eyes closed, he held on to the very last threads of his control before letting them go. He soared even higher, the light disappearing completely, with stars flashing behind his eyes before he tumbled back down and into Sawyer's arms.

Sawyer held him as Randall shook, trying to get enough air into his lungs. Once his body calmed, he rolled over to get closer to Sawyer. "I just need a minute and…."

"No need," Sawyer whispered. "Everything is perfect just as it is right now." He stroked the hair out of Randall's eyes and then gently kissed him. "All is good, and you ain't got to worry about anything."

"Okay." He closed his eyes once again, dozing for a little while until a growl filled the cabin, and Randall groaned as he realized it was his own stomach. "Sorry."

Sawyer snickered and slowly got out of bed. "With tummy rumbles like that, I think you and I need to get you something to eat." He leaned over the bed and kissed him. "I'd stay in here all day if I could."

"Me too," Randall said softly, watching Sawyer's taut body as he headed to the bathroom. He couldn't help sighing at how stunning he was. As soon as the door closed, Randall got out of bed, grabbed his bag, and pulled on clean clothes. By the time Sawyer came out, he was dressed, and Sawyer did the same as he took care of business.

"Where are we going today?" Randall asked.

"The Jackson area. It's a pretty amazing place. It's a place where a lot of stars make their homes. The town is one of those anomalies out here. Real estate is sky high, and estates outside of town are often measured in hundreds of acres. But there are some amazing views, and if we have time, we could head to Jackson. The ski area is closed this time of year, but some of the lifts are running, and you can go to the top of the mountains for some pretty spectacular views. Then tonight we can return to the cabin before making the return trip to the ranch in a day or so."

"Sounds like a great plan, as long as you don't mind doing the driving." He grabbed his things for the day along with a couple bottles of water and followed Sawyer to the truck. He hadn't been able to see it last night, but the trees around the cabin made the entire area seem so remote, and yet five minutes later, they were on the road heading south. "You'd never know the cabins were here."

"That's the beauty of it. Kyle, the owner, rents them out mostly through Airbnb, but I just called him, and he happened to have one available. We got lucky for this time of the year. They're usually pretty full."

The drive to Jackson was almost as spectacular as their trip the day before, with an amazing view almost everywhere he looked.

The town of Jackson was rustic and yet beautiful. "This is most definitely a western town. The bars are themed around cowboys mostly, and they have mechanical bulls and things like that." Sawyer continued driving, turning a corner before they came to a park.

"What is that?"

Sawyer laughed. "The antler arches. There's one on each corner of the park. It's a tradition in this town dating back decades. The arches are big enough to walk under." He parked, and Randall got out. He wasn't sure if he was impressed or appalled, but Sawyer explained that they came from the Boy Scouts who collected dropped antlers in the elk refuge. That made him feel better as he walked around the park, taking pictures of each of the four arches.

"This is so unique," he told Sawyer after seeing each of them.

"Like I said, this was an old, rough-and-tumble town. Now it's very gentrified, but it didn't used to be. The people here made their living off the land, and they were as rugged and craggy as the mountains. There are tons of stories." Sawyer led him into one of the bars. "This one serves a really good breakfast."

Randall leaned close. "After last night, I think I deserve two."

Sawyer's eyes seemed to dance as he pulled open the door, and they went in and took a seat at one of the booths along the side.

"What's your poison, darlin'?" the server asked as she pulled out her pad and a pen. Randall almost answered that it was the guy across the table, but he managed to keep it inside.

"YOU WANT to go on that?" Randall asked as they stood in line near the ski lodge. He could just imagine the activity in winter, with everyone bundled up against the cold, skis slung over shoulders, excitement filling the cold mountain air. He'd been skiing in Switzerland and knew the routine, but he could just imagine this place would be more raw, less genteel and mannered. Maybe he needed to return in the winter and check it out. For a second, he wondered if Sawyer could ski. But standing at the base of the tram, looking up toward the top, gave him pause. "It's a long way."

"Come on," Sawyer said as the line moved forward. "Are you scared of heights?"

"No." He just wasn't sure about going up in that thing with only what looked like a string to keep it in the air. He always had this hesitancy at times like this, but he pushed it aside. "But it should be fine." He hated to admit any sort of weakness. His father had taught him that. If he showed any sign of being weak or scared, his father always picked up on it, and then he'd be punished. At school, things hadn't been much better, with the other boys pouncing at the first indication of insecurity. He stood straighter, determined to power his way through.

"We don't have to do this. I thought you'd like to go to the top. It's supposed to be a great view. At least that's what I've heard."

Randall smiled and nodded. "It should be great," he lied. They inched forward, and Sawyer reached the front of the line for tickets. They got the last pair for a ride to the top in half an hour, which gave Randall thirty minutes to wonder and worry. He hated that he felt this way, and yet he was not going to miss the chance to see from the top just because he was nervous about going up in the lift tram.

He watched as the group before them filed inside and then the lift slipped out of the station on its way up the mountain. "What's got you so tense?" Sawyer asked. "And don't tell me you're not worried. The lines around your eyes and mouth are deeper than the crags on that peak over there."

"I don't like ski lifts, okay?" he admitted grudgingly. He should have been able to power through it. Weakness wasn't something he wanted to show to anyone. "Usually it's not too bad, but I went on a ski lift in Chamonix, France, with my parents when I was a kid. They skied there every winter, and I practically begged to go along. I must have been ten, and my mother gave in. My father wasn't too happy about it, but we had a good time. Everything was great, and even my dad and I got along. We went skiing together and kind of connected." It seemed like the one time he'd really gotten along with his father. They actually had something in common.

He swallowed hard and took a deep breath before releasing it slowly. "My father showed me how to ski down the various hills, and I remember him smiling. We had a good time. Until we got on the lift. We made it halfway to the top and then it stopped. My father and I swung back and forth in the wind, which seemed to grow colder. I remember leaning closer to him just as the lift lurched. I thought we were going to fall, and I grabbed for my father. I must have screamed, because I was ten…." He sighed and bit his lower lip. "My father tensed, and the next thing I know, one of his skis had fallen off into the area below the lift."

"And your father got angry," Sawyer said with a nod. "I've said it before. Your father was an ass."

"Yeah, and he was also an earl, so everyone deferred to his idiocy." He shook his head slowly. "I've never told anyone about this before." He realized he didn't mind Sawyer knowing his history or that he was nervous about the situation. Sawyer was not his father, and he wasn't going to act the same way or use it against him.

"Did he get his ski back?" Sawyer asked.

"One of the ski patrol went up, skied down to it, and brought it to him. He got angry but ended up having coffee in the chalet at the top of the mountain while he waited. As an adult, I can see it wasn't that big a deal, but you'd have thought I stabbed him or something."

The tram returned, and it was their turn to board. They got inside, and the attendant closed the door behind their group. Everyone spent the time looking out the windows as they rose along the side of the mountain. They weren't that high, and the land slid along under them. Randall breathed deeply, trying to concentrate on the view rather than where he was.

"Hey. It's okay," Sawyer whispered. "Look over there. You should see the Teton peaks start to come into view."

Sure enough, as they started to reach the top, the vista opened up and the view nearly took his breath away. It was like they were on top of the world. As they reached the station, the tram slowed, and they got out and wandered onto the deck, where the entire area was laid out below them.

"You can see the town over there."

"It's… wow…," Randall said as he scanned all around, taking in the view from every direction. "I'm glad I came." He had been so close to backing out, but this was worth the discomfort. "I needed to face that old fear." It was long past time that he worked through the issues with his father.

Sawyer slipped his arm around his waist, and they stood together.

"Geez. Can't we go anywhere without seeing that?" a man said from behind them. Randall turned to see an older man with salt-and-pepper hair flopping everywhere, his upper lip curled in a sneer.

"Gerald," the woman next to him said softly, trying to pull him away, "there's no need to make a scene."

"But they're…. It's unnatural."

Sawyer stilled next to him, and Randall shook his head before turning to the side. "Are all Americans this ridiculous?" he asked in his thickest accent. "We were doing nothing but enjoying the view." He seethed on the inside but kept his outward appearance cool.

"But I don't want this… gay stuff"—he waved at them—"in my view."

"Then go over there." Randall waved right back. "Bugger off." He grinned because he'd made a joke, and the yokel in front of him seemed to have no idea. Still, he stormed toward the other side the area, and Randall returned his attention to Sawyer.

"That was interesting."

Randall shrugged. "Nobody is going to give us grief for who we are. Certainly not someone like him." He turned to glare at the man, who had been watching him but looked away as soon as he saw Randall. "I don't understand people like that. They want to stick their noses in our business but would hate it if we did the same thing." He shivered. "Though I do not want to even think about him after the lights go out."

"Yeah. Let's not go there." They turned back to the view, and after a while, made their way back to the line for the tram to return them to the bottom. The middle-aged man and his wife were just ahead of them in line, and Randall did his best to ignore than. Thankfully, they got on the ride down before Randall and Sawyer, and that was last they saw of them.

The return trip was much easier than the one up, and once they reached the ground, Randall and Sawyer headed to town for lunch before meandering back toward the cabin, stopping for plenty of pictures along the way. Randall kept wondering how things were going back at the ranch and whether Sawyer's father had put in another appearance. Their phones had been quiet, but other than in and around Jackson, they didn't have cell service, so it was hard to tell. Still, Randall hoped everything was okay.

"We can stop right up ahead," Sawyer said before pulling off for pictures. The lake and the way it reflected the peaks was amazing. Randall sent a few pictures to friends back home, knowing they would transmit once he had service.

"I almost don't want to go back," Randall said.

"To the ranch…?"

Randall shrugged. "To the ranch, but also back home." He called it home, but it didn't really feel much like it most of the time. The estate still felt like his father's, which was why he spent a great deal of his time in London. "I like it out here. I didn't really think I would."

"How so? Did you think of yourself as a city kind of person?"

Randall shrugged as he thought. "I don't know. I didn't fit in anywhere, but I always thought I was happiest in London. I guess I didn't really settle in there either." He had to admit that being on the ranch with everyone—having them accept him for who he was and not sucking up to him because he was the Earl of Plymouth—felt good.

CHAPTER 10

RAIN ON the cabin roof woke Sawyer in the middle of the night. He groaned and listened to the soft sound above him.

"What's got you worried?" Randall asked. "Is it the rain?"

"No. We always need it this time of year." He closed his eyes. "I keep wondering what sort of mess my father has gotten me into." He rolled over and slid his hand over Randall's bare chest. "It seems like both of us really hit the lottery when it came to fathers."

"Yeah," Randall breathed and tugged him closer. "And there's bugger all you can do about it." He yawned. "Have you heard anything from anyone?"

"No. Alan has been silent, and I figured if someone had showed up, he'd have said something. But I keep wondering if something's wrong and they aren't telling me."

"I doubt that. And I get the feeling that if there had been a lot of drama, Chip would have let you know, if no one else. He doesn't seem like the type to keep news to himself."

"That's true." Still, Sawyer wondered what his father was going to pull. It wasn't like him to just give up, especially when his own skin was on the line. He would be out to try to find a way to get the heat off and shift it to someone else. "We'll find out tomorrow either way." He snuggled closer to Randall and did his best to let the soft sound of the rain lull him to sleep. It didn't work at first, but eventually he drifted off, only to wake with the sun the way he always did. It was the cowboy in him.

Randall was sound asleep, so he slipped out of bed and used the bathroom as quietly as he could. When he came out, Randall was sitting up, Sawyer's cowboy hat plopped on his head. "I was just trying it on for size. What do you think?"

Sawyer strode over lifted the hat off him and plopped it on his own head.

Randall grinned. "Looks better on you." He tugged Sawyer down into a kiss. Sawyer lifted the hat off his head to place it aside. "Leave it on," Randall growled, pulling him down into a steamy kiss.

AFTER LEAVING the cabin in the woods behind, Sawyer missed it. The last few days and nights had been magical, having Randall all to himself without the push and pull of the rest of the ranch and the world. Largely they had been by themselves, and now Sawyer was going to have to share Randall again, and he didn't want to. Sawyer was a cowboy, and his life was close to the land, with the horses. He wasn't someone who longed to be part of the great big world. His own piece of it was just fine with him. And now that they were returning, Sawyer knew that the rest of the world was going to call Randall away.

He couldn't stay here and just be with Sawyer any more than George could have stayed with Alan. The two of them lived in England, and from all indications Alan had a great life. But Alan Justice was one of those men who could make a life for himself anywhere. He was personable, smart, and people liked him… most of the time. Sawyer wasn't like that. He was quiet and preferred to have his life the same way. He didn't long for adventure, and he wasn't interested in shaking everything up. Besides, he could see Alan in England charming the locals. He wasn't going to be able to do that.

"You've been quiet for quite a while. What's bothering you?" Randall asked.

"Nothing important," he told him, because there was no need dumping his stupidness on Randall. They came from two different worlds, and Randall was part of something that he would never fit into. Heck, he'd probably embarrass Randall the first time he had to sit down at one of those fancy dinners he probably had to attend. No, as much as Sawyer might let himself dream, at the end of the week, Alan, George, and Randall would be going back to England, and he'd still be here.

Sawyer had always known that would happen. He thought he had accepted it, but after getting close to Randall, he had known the separation was going to come at a cost. Sawyer also knew that if he'd been given the choice, he wouldn't change anything. The time he got with Randall was a gift, and he was going to be happy with it.

"You can stop brooding," Randall told him. "I know what you're doing. We're going back, and now that our time alone is gone, you're wondering about what's next."

Sawyer sighed. "I know you have to go back home." There was nothing more to say. Facts were what they were, and it was futile to fight against it. That was the very definition of making yourself unhappy: wanting something you couldn't have. No matter how much he might wish for something, that didn't change reality.

"Yes, I do. I have responsibilities there, and as much as my father only did what he felt he wanted to, I have to do better. The people on the estate deserve that. They put up with a lot over the years, and I have to…." He paused and grew quiet.

"What?"

"I have to be the earl they deserve. My father was the kind of person who only liked the noblesse part of our role. But I have an obligation to them. I haven't lived up to that very well. At least until now." Sawyer turned to glance at Randall, who looked back at him with determination. "I mean, I've spent a lot of my time away from the estate. I take the money it brings in and use it to live the kind of life I want, like my dad did, but…." He paused again. "I don't want to turn into him."

"Then don't," Sawyer told him. "It's not that hard. Just figure out what your father would have done… and do something different. You know he was an ass and self-centered, so don't be that way." It seemed simple enough to him.

"It's not that easy." Randall looked at him like he was dumb, and Sawyer gripped the wheel more tightly.

"Yes, it is. You can be whoever you want to be. So if you truly want to be different from your father, then you will. But if you are only saying that you want to be different and you really want the same kind of easy life he had, then you'll do that. People say they want to change all the time, but what they really mean is that they want others to think they've changed so they can do the same things they always have."

Randall ran a hand through his hair. "Is that what you really think of me?" His eyes grew wider. "You really can be an ass sometimes."

Sawyer shrugged. "It goes with the job, I guess. Living out here, we don't have time for the niceties or beating around the bush. We get to it and talk straight. But think about it. You worked hard on the ranch, and you did all the shit jobs I gave you. I know you lost a bet, but you did them anyway. You aren't afraid of hard work. So no, I don't think that. But what I think isn't what's important. It's what you think about yourself. That's what counts."

"Huh?"

"Yeah. You worked hard. So if you work as hard for yourself and for the people who depend on you, then you'll be a success. On a ranch it's all about what you put into it. Claude, and Mrs. Justice are all really successful, and they work hard every day to help bring that about. So you do the same and see if things don't change back home. And when you do leave, you can call me if you want and I'll always tell you the truth." It hurt to talk about him going, but it was just a matter of days. He was going to have to get used to it.

THE RANCH came into sight a few hours later. Sawyer was excited to be home and pulled into the yard. He didn't know what to expect when they returned, but the place was quiet—unusually so. "Where is everyone?" Randall asked.

"I have no idea," Sawyer said as he opened his door. "I'm going to check the barn. You go inside the house and see if anyone is around." He climbed out and hurried into the barn. The horses inside the barn greeted him from their stalls. They all had hay and water. Sawyer checked the ones out in the paddocks, and they all seemed fine. The colts greeted him, looking for treats.

Nothing seemed out of place, and yet he got the feeling that something wasn't right. He returned to the inside of the barn and found a strange man standing in the center.

"We've been looking for you."

"What do you want?" Sawyer asked, already tensing at the intimidation the man exuded. He was about six feet, over two hundred pounds, with a crooked nose and eyes as cold as January. He was most definitely not the kind of guy you'd want to meet in a deserted alley—or a stable for that matter.

"Your family owes us a lot of money, and I'm here to collect," he said as levelly as if he were giving the weather report on television.

"I don't owe you anything. My father does, and you can collect from that deadbeat yourself. I don't have what he owes you, and I'm not paying his debts. So you can go barking up another tree. There's no blood in this turnip." He was already so angry at his father that he wanted to beat the shit out of him.

"He's disappeared, but we know where you are, and there are plenty of things we can do to make you want to pay us." He sneered.

Sawyer rolled his eyes. "Do you really think that's going to work? What are you, some character in a bad mob movie?" He stepped forward, pulling out his phone. He dialed 911, and it connected. "Send the sheriff to the Justice ranch right away," he said as soon as the call connected. "Did you hear me?"

"Yes," the operator said before Sawyer's phone flew from his hand and landed on one of the bales of straw nearby, his hand aching from the slap.

"You're going to regret that."

"Why don't you pick on someone else?" Randall said from behind him. The bruiser turned as a truck pulled into the yard, followed by a second one. "It seems you're outnumbered."

With Randall now in front of him and Sawyer behind, the bruiser looked back at him and then returned his attention to Randall. He must have figured he stood a better chance with him. The bruiser took a swing at Randall and missed as he dodged. Randall countered and got the guy square in the nose. Sawyer heard the crunch as it broke. Maybe if they set it right this time, it would improve his looks.

"Jesus," the bruiser groaned as he covered his face, blood streaking through his fingers.

Randall attacked again, this time catching the guy in the gut. He doubled over, gasping for breath, but Randall wasn't done. He used both hands together to snap him in the back, bringing him flat on the ground. "Don't move or I'll break your bloody neck." Randall stepped back, probably in case the guy decided to try anything.

"You broke my nose," he mumbled.

"It's an improvement. Now stay down," Randall snapped. "Don't make me kick you in the head until you pass out, because I will."

"What happened?" Alan asked as he and George hurried into the barn. They came to a stop near the prone man, looking at Randall with a touch of awe.

"Where were all of you?"

"A huge section of fence was down. We had to get it back up before the herd spread halfway across the county." He put his hands on his hips.

"The fences were damaged, and I'm willing to bet this idiot was the one who did it."

"That's cattle rustling and destruction of property," George said with a smile. "You know, they kill people around here for less than that. String them up from the nearest tree and let the birds peck at them." Sawyer bit his lower lip to keep from laughing as the guy on the ground began to shake. "I saw it last year. It wasn't pretty. After the coyotes and wolves were through, there was nothing left." The guy shook harder as a siren drew closer.

The bruiser tried again to get up as more of the men joined them in the barn, forming a ring around him that parted as the sheriff and a deputy strode in. "Please don't let these people get to me," the bruiser begged. The sheriff turned to Alan, who did his best to look innocent.

"All right. We'll take you back to town and put you in a nice, safe jail cell." He smirked as he cuffed the man and got him to his feet. "Don't bleed all over my car," he added before getting him into the back seat. He left the deputy to watch over the suspect and returned. "What did you tell him?" he demanded of Alan.

"It wasn't me. George told him a whopper that scared the crap out of him. I thought he was going to mess himself." He tugged George to his side.

"He threatened me for payment," Sawyer said.

"And I believe he ran down a section of fence that we had to replace," Alan added. "So add attempted rustling and destruction of property to the charges. He's probably from out of state, so make sure the judge knows this guy will run if he gets out on bail."

The sheriff narrowed his gaze at Alan. "I'm well aware of how to do my job."

"We only want to make sure you have all the facts," George said. "He threatened Sawyer."

The sheriff approached Sawyer, and he explained everything that he said. He also told him how the bruiser threw the first punch and that Randall had done nothing more than make sure he was down and didn't hurt anyone.

"It seemed as though he might have gone a little overboard," the sheriff said. "He looks beaten to hell, and you don't have a scratch on you."

"I caught him in the nose and then the belly. It seemed to me that he was going to try to attack again, so I made sure he ended up on the ground. Other than his nose, I didn't break any bones, and I certainly could have. As it is, if he gets it set correctly, he'll come out of it better off than he went in." Randall shrugged. "Either way, it was self-defense. He was the one making threats. We simply neutralized him."

The sheriff made notes.

"Also, where is his vehicle? It has to be around here. He cut the fence to get everyone away, so what was he planning? We had been gone and just got home, so he had no idea if we were here or not."

"Sheriff, do you want me to run the suspect into town? I can return to pick you up," the deputy said.

"You book him and get him in a cell. Call Doc Harper and have him give him a look over once he's secure. I'll call in and request backup. I can ride in with them."

"Will do," the deputy said and got back in the car, taking off with the sirens blaring. The sheriff called in with his request for backup and then took a walk down the drive. Sawyer went along with him.

"The guy couldn't have walked over here," the sheriff said.

"Sheriff," Sawyer said and led him to the stable area, pointing out a set of keys against the wall of the second stable. "You're probably looking for these." The sheriff pulled on gloves and pressed the red panic button, and a horn began to sound. "Just over here." He led the way to a depression in the road where a black SUV had been parked, its lights now flashing. The sheriff silenced the vehicle and Sawyer stayed behind him as they approached the vehicle.

He waited while the sheriff went through the inside and pulled out a can of gasoline from the very back. "Do you think he intended to use that?" He turned toward the ranch buildings.

"Don't know. He'll say it was just extra fuel, but I doubt that. The gas tank is nearly full. My guess would be that he'd set a fire to send a message that he meant business."

Sawyer figured he was right. "What can you do?"

"When I get back to the office in town, I'll talk to him, but I doubt I'll get anything out of him. He'll lawyer up pretty fast once he calls his boss. But I'll watch his calls, and maybe we can find out who he works for. Not that it's going to do him a lot of good. He isn't going to be let loose. Judge Walker doesn't look kindly on troublemakers like him."

"That's good to know. But you can never tell. They'll probably send him some high-powered lawyer who is going to try to run circles around everyone."

"Maybe and maybe not." He backed out of the truck. "Other than the gas, there is nothing in here that tells us anything." He closed the door. "I'll have it towed in tomorrow. I'm going to need you and your English friend to come in and give statements. And we'll come out to see if we can get any physical evidence off the fencing that he cut. If we can put him there, then we have direct evidence of vandalism and property destruction."

"If there's anything we can do...." Sawyer wanted to put this behind him if possible. "Should Randall and I follow you into town to give our statements?"

"That would be good." They walked back toward the ranch buildings as another deputy pulled into the drive. He picked up the sheriff, who went to do his job while Sawyer got Randall so they could get their statements taken.

"Is that all there is to it?" Randall asked two hours later as they left the sheriff's office.

"For us, I guess," Sawyer said. "The sheriff doesn't think he'll be granted bail, but you never know. At least what we gave them should help." He hoped so. The last thing he wanted was for this guy to get loose and threaten him again. Not that he had any illusions that this little episode was the last he was going to hear about it. But he had also sent a message that going after him was not going to be a walk in the park. He supposed that was the best he could do.

"We'll see." Sawyer got in the truck and Randall did the same as one of the deputies hurried down the steps and out to where they were about to leave.

He lowered the window. "Is there a problem?"

"The suspect we brought in says he wants to bring charges against Randall."

"Can he do that?" Sawyer grew nervous. That was all he needed.

The deputy shrugged. "I suppose he can try, but he swung first, and that makes it self-defense. It isn't going to go anywhere, but the sheriff asked me to make sure you knew. He said he'll take care of it."

"Good."

"But please don't go anywhere until this is cleared up," the deputy said.

"I'm supposed to catch a flight home on Saturday, so tell the sheriff he has until then to clear up whatever he needs to. After that I have to get back."

The deputy leaned closer. "The sheriff is the law around here—"

Randall shook his head. "That isn't how it works here or back home. The law is the law, and he's bound by it. I was defending myself and Sawyer… along with everyone else on the ranch. I have witnesses, and nothing is going to change that. So like I said, please inform the sheriff that he has until Saturday. Otherwise I will be leaving, and he can discuss it with Mrs. Justice."

Sawyer bit back a chuckle. Dealing with Mrs. J was the last thing the sheriff wanted—she had his number. "Thank you, Deputy. I'm sure everything will be straightened out by then." He raised the windows and pulled out of the lot.

"The sheriff has a lot of authority here. There are courts and judges, but a lot of them live in other towns. So being in jail can mean days before seeing a judge at all. In the meantime, it's the sheriff who calls the shots."

Randall snickered. "Except with Mrs. J."

"Yeah. Except with her. Everyone knows that she has a lot of sway with folks in town, and neither the sheriff nor any other elected official wants to be on her bad side." They pulled out of town, the lights receding behind them. Sawyer hated to think about the fact that Randall was leaving in a matter of days. Everything had changed for him in such a short period of time. Sawyer had always thought he was one of those people who was better off alone. But Randall had changed all that. Yeah, he could go back to the way things had been, but the idea didn't appeal. It had been nice to have someone to do things with. Alan and George always went riding together. They often camped out or took road trips together, just the two of them. Sawyer hadn't really thought about it, but now he wanted what they had. Somone to talk with, take trips with, ride with, sleep with, and know was there for him. Still, he couldn't ask Randall to stay. There was nothing for him here, and he had duties to the folks back home. If he convinced Randall to stay, he'd be no better than his father, and Sawyer knew Randall was a much better person than the man who sired him. There was no way around it—Randall had to go home. Sawyer was going to need to get used to being alone and doing things on his own once more.

CHAPTER 11

"HE WANTS to talk to you," the sheriff said the following morning after wandering into the barn to find Randall working with Sawyer.

"Who does?" Sawyer snapped as he set the shovel aside.

Randall leaned his tools with Sawyer's and left the stall to join the sheriff.

"Colton Weaver, the man you beat the crap out of yesterday." He seemed more than a little pleased at the idea, now that he had all the facts. "I don't want you making a habit of it, but you sure you wouldn't like to be a deputy?" Damn, what a difference a day made. "He wants to see both of you, actually. I think he realizes that his charges aren't going away and that he's in deep legal shit, especially once I was able to get his criminal history. He's wanted in Arizona as well as Nevada, so he's pretty much up a creek, no paddle."

"Do we have to?" Sawyer asked.

Randall moved closer, slipping an arm around Sawyer's waist. He glanced at the sheriff, who tensed but said nothing. "No, you don't. Neither of us owes him anything. He came here, caused mischief, and was most likely intent on giving us a demonstration, based on the gasoline you found. That kind of person is owed nothing."

"True," the sheriff agreed with him. "But he may have something to tell you. I don't know, but it isn't going to hurt to talk to him. He won't be in the same area as you and isn't going to leave his cell. I'll have a deputy with you, standing nearby, so if he tries anything, we can handle it."

Sawyer turned to him, and Randall met his worried gaze. "You don't need to, but I think I will. I want to hear what he has to say for himself, and I want him to know that he got the tar beat out of him by a gay man. Let him stew on that."

"Do we have to see him alone?" Sawyer asked.

"Nope."

Sawyer nodded. "Okay. I'll see what he wants, but whatever it is, this is not privileged information. I want cameras, and I want it recorded. If he admits to anything, then amend the charges."

"Agreed," the sheriff told him. "Let's go and get his over with."

Sawyer sighed. "All right. We'll follow you into town." He wiped his hands and left the barn.

"Aren't you going to change your boots?" Randall asked.

"Nah. They're covered in manure. I think that's appropriate." He left, and Randall followed him out and climbed into the truck.

The sheriff drove like a bat out of hell, and they kept right up with him until they pulled into the lot and parked next to his patrol car. They followed him inside and through a series of locked doors to the cells. A deputy unlocked one of them and followed them inside. The bruiser paced the neighboring cell like a caged animal.

He stopped, approaching the bars, but said nothing at first. "You wanted to talk to us." The snarl was almost silent, but there. "Say what you want to say or we're leaving," Randall told him. They weren't going to waste time with this guy. Still he stared that them as if trying to intimidate them, but it wasn't going to work. "Fine."

"It isn't going to work, you know," the bruiser finally said. "Keeping me here. It isn't going to stop anything. They'll just send someone else."

Randall rolled his eyes. "And you're telling us this out of the goodness of your heart? Who are they? Some nameless presence that controls everything? I don't believe in crap like that." He glanced at Sawyer, who seemed content to let him do the talking. "I know you want something, and we have nothing to give you. Your employer can get you all the fancy lawyers they want, but you're going to be tried from state to state, and I doubt you'll see the light of day until you're old and gray."

Sawyer moved closer. "What is it you want?" Randall crossed his arms over his chest while Sawyer spoke more gently. "I know you were doing a job for someone else."

"Doesn't matter."

"Maybe not. But you wanted to talk to me, and I'm here. You specifically asked, and I came, so what is it you wanted to say? This is the only chance you're going to get."

The bruiser shifted his weight slightly, not moving his gaze from Sawyer. But he went quiet like he was thinking about what he wanted to do. "Then let's go," Randall snapped and began herding Sawyer toward the door. "We've wasted enough time with him." He'd gladly play the hardass if it got them some results.

"Your father owes some really nasty people a lot of money, and they aren't going to stop trying to collect it."

Sawyer shrugged. "Then they can have him. I don't care. He was a shit father, and I don't owe him a single thing. So you tell your people when they show up that if they were counting on me paying his debt, they're barking up the wrong tree. I don't have that kind of money, and in case you haven't seen it, the local sheriff and his deputies as well as half the town are behind us. There is nothing secret here. He can try to send someone else like you, but we'll form a fucking army and hunt them down." Sawyer was magnificent.

"You think so? Mr. Calderone isn't someone to mess with," the bruiser spat, and then almost gasped when he realized he'd let a name slip.

Randall didn't react to it. "If all you have are threats and attempts to scare us, you are really stupid. We don't care." He drew closer but stayed out of reach in case he tried something. "You took a swing at me, and I took you down to the ground. It wasn't that hard. So anyone else he sends will end up the same way. We gay people learned a long time ago how to fight our own battles, and one way or another, we win them." He turned away, taking Sawyer's hand. "Come on. It's time to go. All we're getting is the same regurgitated crap." He nodded to the deputy, who opened the door, and they stepped out and left the cell area of the building.

"Well, that was useless," Sawyer said.

"No, it wasn't," Randall said as the sheriff come over. "We got a name. I don't think he meant to say it, but we got Calderone out of him. Does that mean anything to you?" he asked. Both the sheriff and the deputy shook their heads.

"Then get on whatever database of bad guys you have and see what you can find. I bet I could find out things by googling him." It seemed Randall was taking a page from Mrs. J. "See what you can find, please."

"We will," the sheriff told him gruffly.

"Thank you." It seemed that Randall didn't care if he goaded the sheriff into doing his job or not, just as long as he did what he wanted. "We appreciate all your help," he added with those butter-wouldn't-melt-in-his-mouth manners.

"Can we head back to the ranch now?" Sawyer asked. The sheriff nodded and then asked one of the deputies to see them out.

SAWYER WAS quiet the entire ride back to the ranch. He looked out the windows, keeping whatever was racing through his mind to himself.

He wasn't in any mood to talk, and he figured Randall knew him well enough to understand that when Sawyer had something on his mind, he grew quiet. Once they pulled into the ranch drive and parked, Sawyer went right to the barn without a word. Randall hesitated behind him, probably wondering if he should follow.

Eventually he charged into the barn. "Okay. What's going on in that head of yours?" he asked, picking up the shovel he'd set aside earlier.

"Nothing," Sawyer told him.

"Bullshit," Randall countered. "You get quiet when you get moody and stuck in your head. So spill it. You will eventually, so just get it over with." Sawyer tensed at Randall's bull-in-a-china-shop routine.

"You were pushy in there, with everyone. Even the sheriff," Sawyer told him, more confused than angry. "You came off as an ass."

"Yeah, I know. What did you think I was going for?" He held Sawyer's pissed-off gaze. "That was the plan. I act like a dick, and you be the good guy. And it worked. He told you something he didn't mean to. Now the sheriff can do some research and we'll know who we're dealing with, and the sheriff can go after him." It may have worked, but Randall's actions really triggered something inside him.

"It is that simple for you?" Sawyer asked. "Are you that good at getting people to do what you want them to, or is that part of your upbringing and you just expect people to do what you want?"

Randall shook his head, blinking. "You think this has something to do with who I am? That I'm an earl? Here in the US, that means nothing. You and the folks at the ranch taught me that. I've been here ten days, and no one has treated me any differently than anyone else except for the fact that I'm a guest of Alan and George's. Remember, you gave me a great deal of grief when I first got here, so my position didn't mean a fig to you." He shrugged. "Do you think the sheriff cares?"

Sawyer took a step back. "No. I guess I'm being sensitive or something." The truth was that he wasn't looking forward to the disappointment that was sure to come his way, and all the talk of Randall leaving got under his skin. He knew that there was nothing he could do about it, but it bothered him. He hated it when things were out of his control, and lately it seemed like everything was. "You did good today. But what I want to know is what the sheriff or anyone thinks they can do. If this Calderone is as bad as I think he is, then he'll just send someone else to try to pressure me to pay off my father's debt. I won't be pressured, and I can't pay it anyhow. I don't have that kind of money." Sawyer turned to Randall, seeing something in his eyes.

"Well, I have resources, and—"

Sawyer shook his head. "No. I'm not going to pay my useless father's debts, and I can't let someone else do it either. His bad behavior and irresponsibility are his own. They aren't yours or mine. Let them take their debt out of his hide. Someone has to make him suffer the consequences of his actions. If I pay it off, he'll just go back to his old ways. In fact, I would be surprised if he isn't off gambling somewhere else with money he doesn't have."

"Okay. Then what do you want to do?" Randall asked.

"I don't know. I'll figure it out. You're going home this weekend, and after that I'll have to see what options are open to me. It may be time for me to move on. That way I won't be putting anyone else here in danger."

"Just yourself," Randall told him. "You're going to be on your own and vulnerable. As long as you're here…."

"Then Mrs. J, Chip, and the rest of the hands are in the line of fire. George and Alan will be gone as well, and these people are too good for me to put them in danger. To let my father do that."

"But you'd also be letting your father upend your life," Randall said, and all Sawyer could do was shrug. His father had done that more than once, and he hated the thought of him doing it again, but there was nothing he could do about it. His father was his cross to bear, and he wasn't going to let his life and family affect the others around him.

"We should get back to work." He really didn't want to keep talking about this. It was like his family business had been opened up and put out for the entire world to examine, and he hated it.

"Fine. But we will talk about this again. You can't put me off that easily." Randall got busy, and Sawyer watched him for a minute, wondering why that notion made his belly warm.

"WHAT CAN we do for you, Sheriff?" Sawyer heard Alan ask from outside. He groaned because he knew that this visit was all about him and the mess his father had made.

"It's okay," Randall said from near him. "Alan is a big boy, and he can certainly handle anything."

"You know, if this affects anyone here, then it affects me and my family as well," Alan said flatly.

"It's best if I speak directly with Sawyer, but you all should hear what I have to say," he added as Sawyer joined them in the yard, Randall behind him. Somehow he knew that he'd be there without Sawyer having to ask.

"What's going on? Is there any change with your guest?"

The sheriff shook his head. "Other than his lawyer showing up, making a ton of demands, and getting them shot down by the judge as fast as he could make them. That man is not going anywhere, and they're pissing up the wrong pole if they think otherwise." It was good to see the sheriff so worked up. It gave him some hope.

"I assume that isn't the reason you came all the way out here," Sawyer said. "You may as well give us the bad news." He steadied himself.

"Well… I was able to get information on a Vincent Calderone, and he is nothing but bad news. He was part owner of a pair of casinos in the south but was forced out because of his spurious business connections. But apparently he still has his hand on the back door, and it seems your father borrowed money from him or one of his men. Vincent is connected, in a big way, and he isn't going to just walk away from any debt. It would make him look weak, and that is something he could never allow."

"Great. So what do I do?"

Randall cleared his throat. "Come home with me. There's plenty of space, and you'll be out of the country. He can look for you all he wants, but he isn't going to get his hands on you there. His people aren't even going to be able to get into the country. If they have any sort of record, they'll be denied entry. You'll be out of their reach."

"Mom can tell anyone who asks that you quit and left. You'll be safe, and so will everyone here."

"It's a good idea," the sheriff agreed. "There are plenty of ways to reinforce the idea, and once the threat has passed, you can come back. It's not like you did anything wrong." He seemed pleased, which pissed Sawyer off. Like he was letting everyone else do his job for him.

"I'd love for you to come," Randall said.

Sawyer shook his head. "I'm not going to run from this. I'm not some coward." He hated that the others thought that, and he couldn't face them at the moment. He went back into the barn, pulling the door closed after him, hoping to all hell that everyone would just leave him alone.

He worked for hours, cleaning every stall, sweeping, and dusting down the tack room. He also hosed down the concrete in the center of the barn and swept away any dirt. The place was as spotless as a barn could get by the time he was through. He had so much angry energy, and he just had to wear it off.

Eventually the barn door slid open and Randall clomped down the aisle in his new boots. He got some tack and saddled the horse he'd ridden before. He also saddled Sawyer's horse and led them both out of the barn.

"Where are you going with those?" Sawyer snapped, still on edge.

"We're going riding," Randall told him. "Well, I am. You can either come along or put this guy here back in his stall." He seemed angry, and Sawyer sighed and put his tools away. "It's your choice."

Sawyer found Randall in the yard, holding the reins of both horses. He passed the one set to him and then mounted his horse, waiting for Sawyer.

"Sometimes you are the pushiest person on earth."

"And sometimes you are the biggest pain in the ass. Now get on. We're going." He nudged his horse forward, leaving Sawyer standing alone. The bastard didn't even look back.

Sawyer mounted and hurried to catch up. "You think you won something?"

"Yeah, the booby prize—your prickly company for the next hour." Randall seemed upset, and Sawyer didn't know why. He was the one who everyone wanted to hurry away with his tail between his legs. It was one thing when leaving was his choice. But he had decided to stay, and now everyone, including Randall, had suddenly changed their tune and wanted him out of here. God, this whole situation sucked, and he really needed to get his head around it. Most of the time it felt like he was revving his engine but only spinning his wheels.

"I'm fine."

"No, you're not," Randall said. "You're angry because we all suggested you leave." He picked up the pace, and Sawyer did the same just to keep up. "You've thought about it. I know you have. So why get all upset?"

"You just don't understand," Sawyer said, wishing he had the words to explain.

Randall chuckled. "Maybe I do and maybe I don't. But you'll never know until you talk to me."

"Smartass," Sawyer retorted.

"Fine." Randall took off, and Sawyer groaned before following him, his horse flying over the range land, his hair blowing in the wind. There was nothing as invigorating or mind-clearing as the wind around him and a horse galloping under him. The connection between the two of them was astounding, and it always made Sawyer's heart soar.

As they reached the tree line that indicated the creek that was the water source for the ranch, they slowed and pulled up. Randall dismounted and tied up his horse, waiting for him. Sawyer did the same, then followed Randall under the trees. "Is this some kind of forced march?"

Randall stopped at the edge of the creek, the water gurgling over the stones as it went on its way. "No. It's an effort to get you to pull your head out of your ass. Is it working?" he barked.

"You want me to run away too."

Randall shook his head. "What I want you to do is come back with me. I've seen your world, and I can show you mine. It's so different from this. It's green, really green, because it rains a lot. There are expansive lawns and paddocks. I have a few horses for riding—nothing like what they have here. But it's my home and where I grew up." Randall tugged him close, so they were chest to chest. "I want you to come. I don't want to go back and just say goodbye." He leaned slightly forward, his heated gaze boring into Sawyer's. "I want to see if what we have is some sort of fluke or if it's real."

"Then stay," Sawyer said.

"I can't. You made me see that I need to be a better version of myself, and to do that I have to be there. There are changes I need to make, and dammit, I could use your help to do that. You'd be helping me, and you'd be safe." Randall's voice cracked, and Sawyer found himself nodding.

Randall kissed him hard enough to nearly buckle his knees, only backing away when they needed to come up for air. Then he kissed him again, his hands roaming down Sawyer's back, then holding his ass hard and firm until Sawyer groaned deeply against his lips.

"Okay," he growled. "I'll go back with you since you asked so fucking nicely."

"Good. Now how about we get on to the fucking?" Randall pressed Sawyer down onto the grass, kissing him nearly senseless as he opened his belt and popped the buttons on his jeans.

Chapter 12

It seemed that getting a passport at the last minute was a big deal with many obstacles, not the least of which was the trip to Cheyenne to the federal offices there. Fortunately, Sawyer had a copy of his birth certificate, and they were able to get him a picture. Now they were back in Cheyenne at the airport for their flight to Philadelphia. From there, they would catch their flight to London.

"What are we going to do when we get there?" Sawyer asked as he sat in his seat on the plane, bouncing his leg nervously.

"Have you flown before?" Randall asked, realizing he probably should have asked Sawyer before now. When Sawyer shook his head, Randall took his hand and held it through the announcements and taxiing. Sawyer seemed to hold his breath as soon as they hit the runway, and didn't inhale until they were in the air. "It's okay. Just breathe and relax. We're on our way."

"Jesus," Sawyer said, looking out the window as the ground got farther away and the world seemed to get smaller. "My head feels funny."

"It's the cabin pressure." Randall gave Sawyer some gum, and once they leveled off, he reclined his seat back. "Just relax and take it easy. We have about three hours before we land, and there's plenty of time for us to catch our overnight flight."

"Are you a real cowboy?" the boy from the row in front of them asked as he peered between the seats. "My daddy says you might be."

"He is," Randall answered.

"Really? Do you rope steers and ride bulls?" The kid's eyes grew huge.

"I used to, but I don't anymore. Now I take care of the horses and look after the herd. Do you want to be a cowboy when you grow up?" Sawyer asked.

The kid shook his head, looking down. "Daddy said I can't be one 'cause I got 'plepsy." He probably meant epilepsy. The kid was so cute. He had to be about five and was as curious as anything. "He says I can be a lawyer or a doctor if I want."

Sawyer leaned forward as if sharing a secret. "Kid, you can be whatever you want to be if you want it bad enough and are willing to work on it. I always wanted to be a football player when I grew up. Instead I'm a cowboy."

The kid looked to the side, probably at his dad, and then back through the seat. "A cowboy is better. You get to ride horses."

"Ethan, you need to turn around," his father said and got him settled back in his seat.

Randall lost track of what happened between them after that. But every now and then Ethan and Sawyer would exchange looks between the seats, which was precious, and Randall noticed that Sawyer wasn't nearly as nervous, though he did tense up during the landing and was anxious to get out of the plane once they came to a stop.

As soon as they stepped off the Jetway, Sawyer came to a complete stop. If this had been a comedy, everyone behind them would have smacked into the person in front of them. "What's wrong?"

"Where did all these people come from?" Sawyer asked, taking a few steps forward, staying off to the edge of the airport pandemonium. People hurried from place to place, and announcements followed one after another. Randall tried to see how this looked to a cowboy from Wyoming who was used to open spaces and plenty of fresh air, not this airport chaos.

"It's okay. Think of this as a busy highway. Some of these people are going to their flights, while others are getting off like us. It will be fine. The first thing we need to do is get to the international terminal. There we can check in for our flight to London and get something to eat. All we have to do is go this way."

Sawyer grabbed his carry-on bag, plopped his hat onto his head, and followed Randall through the airport. Occasionally Randall turned to check that he was still there and found folks staring at him. Maybe it was the cowboy swagger, or the way he tipped his hat to the ladies, but Randall pretty much figured it was because Sawyer was the hottest man to walk these halls this year. At least that was his opinion.

"How much longer do we have to wait?" Sawyer asked.

"You have enough time to get a Coke or something," Randall said with a smile. "We'll be among the first to board. But that isn't going to be for half an hour." He settled with his book and their bags while Sawyer went to find something to drink.

"They have all kinds of stuff here."

"It's supposed to be duty-free, but it's usually overpriced."

"I thought so. But I promised Mrs. J that I'd bring her back some really good Scotch whisky. She loves the stuff. And I need to get something for Chip. But I can look while I'm at your home. It will be better." He sat down, stretching out his long legs. "I've never been anywhere before."

"I can tell," Randall said gently. "It's like watching everything through fresh eyes, and there are going to be plenty of other things to see. I can't wait to show you my home and for you to meet the people who live there. We can see London and all the famous sights if you want to."

Sawyer shrugged. "I'll let you show me what you think is interesting. I'm not much for museums and stuff like that. Though I hear the queen used to love her horses. Can we see them?"

"I don't think so. But I'll see what I can come up with to make your visit interesting." When their flight was called, Randall guided Sawyer through the gate check and onto the plane, where they were shown to their business-class seats.

TRAVEL SUCKED, and by the time they reached London and got on the train out of the city, Randall was exhausted. Dang it all, once they got in the air and there hadn't been anything to see, Sawyer had put his feet up, reclined his seat, and slept the entire trip over the Atlantic. Randall spent most of the time reading and being a little jealous of Sawyer's ability to rest on a plane. It was something he had never mastered. And now, while he was exhausted and trying to doze, his usually quiet and reserved cowboy was like the Energizer Bunny.

"What is that?"

"Just a small town," Randall answered.

Sawyer plopped his hat on his head and nearly knocked it off again as he tried to get closer to the window. "You weren't kidding. It really is green here." The usual British weather had made an appearance, with clouds growing lower and rain pelting the carriage as they continued the trip. "Does it rain all the time?"

"Not all the time, but it rains a lot. We have plenty of gloomy days like this, so we have plenty of wet-weather gear and don't let a little liquid sunshine stop us."

Sawyer finally stretched out and seemed to relax. "I know I'm being dumb, but I've never been anywhere like this before. Growing up, we never got to go anyplace." He shrugged before turning back to the window. Randall chuckled softly and took Sawyer's hand for a minute, receiving an almost brilliant, excited smile in return. Damn, if a ride in a train got him that kind of reaction, he intended to make sure they took plenty of trips.

"You enjoy yourself. We'll be at our station in a while." He settled back, just happy that Sawyer was enjoying himself and not bored out of his mind. Randall had made this trip a ton of times. Sometimes he drove, but the train was so much easier, especially going into London, where parking was so much trouble.

At the station, Sawyer climbed out of the carriage and got their luggage, hefting the two suitcases while Randall carried the smaller bags. His cowboy stood taller than most people and was easily the talk of everyone he passed. A few times he paused to tip his hat. Eventually they went into the station and out to the street side, where Randall had arranged for a car.

Sawyer insisted on loading the luggage in the boot for the driver and then held the door for Randall. "I take it your mama's manners come out when you're nervous," Randall teased, and Sawyer shrugged.

"How long does it take to get to your house?"

"About ten minutes." Randall settled back, every house and road familiar to him. He had explored them all as a boy, and they hadn't changed much. It was like going to back in time, and he loved it. He had never realized how much until now. He had let his father and his miserable childhood color everything about this place and his life. Taking Sawyer's hand, he realized just how much he owed the man next to him.

"Holy shit," Sawyer swore as the driver pulled into the drive up to the house. "This place is huge." He tilted his head so he could see out the window.

"Yes, I suppose it is." The manicured gardens spread out on both sides of the drive, and in the distance, great lawns met the old estate trees. The gardens, lawns, and forests were all managed and maintained without much help from Randall.

"It looks like something out of a movie," Sawyer said as the car stopped. He bounded out and looked around. Randall stood next to him, trying to see the old Regency-era pile the way Sawyer did. "And the flowers...." Sawyer's voice broke. "My mama would have loved to see this."

"Maybe we should go in and get out of the rain," Randall offered, and Sawyer hefted the bags out of the back before thanking him for the ride and shaking his hand.

"Lead the way," Sawyer said.

Randall climbed the steps and pulled open the tall front door before entering his family home's grand foyer, with its marble floors and rich woodwork. Walls hung with the souvenirs of his ancestors' European grand tours.

"Celeste, this is Sawyer Kincaid. He's going to be staying with me for a while."

"Pleased to meet you." Sawyer set down the bags, pulled off his hat, and made a slight bow of his head.

"Celeste manages the house for me. She makes sure all the tours are running well and that everything in the house is exactly as it should be." Randall smiled. "Is there anything that I should know?"

"There's a tour that's just started. They will be coming this way in about ten minutes. After that they are every half hour, and we close the house at five."

"Then we should leave this portion of the house."

"I'll get someone to bring your bags," Celeste said.

Sawyer lifted the bags. "That's okay, ma'am. They have their work to do, and I can get these. Thank you." He picked up the bags, and Randall went into the library and opened a secret door in the bookcases that led to the private family wing. "Now this is more like it. I don't feel like I'm going to break stuff just by looking at it."

Randall shook his head as he glanced around the room with fresh eyes. The furniture was sturdy but old and well used. Everything in the room, just like the rest of the house, had come down to him from his father. "Make yourself comfortable." Sawyer put down the bags. "I can get us some tea and a few things to eat."

"Okay. Then I want to see the rest of the house and the gardens and the stables. And I want to meet your horses." He went to the windows to look out. "How much land is there?"

"About ten thousand acres. Much of it is leased out to local farmers, and there are about two thousand acres of woodlands that my grandfather was smart enough to protect. My father did nothing with it out of sheer neglect, so the area is quite wild at the moment. I hired a forester who manages that acreage now. Some of it we leave completely wild, and other areas are managed more actively. We thin some of the trees and sell the wood. We're very careful. It's become quite a lucrative business for the estate."

"And what about all these tour people? Do they pay you too? It sounds to me like you got money coming in from all over the place."

Randall sighed. "The house tours help pay for the upkeep on the mansion. I'm happy if they keep the lights on, the place heated, and allow us to do regular maintenance. Right now, we're saving up for a new roof, which is going to be a huge expense. I have about ten years on this one, and it's going to take that long to save up to pay for it. Then there's the estate store, where we sell the things we produce here on the estate, like some of our wool products. We have sheep and goats on the farms. We sell the cheese and goat's milk in the shop. From the sheep, we sell wool for knitting and such and fleece blankets. Some of the villagers use the wool to make hats and jumpers, and we sell those as well. I have a tenant who uses some of the trees we fell to make bowls, spoons, and other wooden implements. Everything in the store has some sort of connection to the estate. My father liked to take credit for the store idea, but it was the estate manager who had the idea and came to my father with it. Jessup is a real visionary. He retired, but he lives in the village. I'll introduce you." Randall cleared his throat. "All that money goes strictly to upkeep. Nothing more."

"So you just take care of the place?"

"Yes and no." Randall put his feet up, and Sawyer finally sat down. "I have an income because my grandfather realized the kind of man his son was and tied up the family money really well. I have income from that trust, and I have some real estate in London that generates income. I try to live off that so the rest can go to the house." Sawyer seemed so restless. "Come on." Randall was tired, but there was no fighting Sawyer's energy. "Let's take a walk." He stood and led Sawyer out of the sitting room and through the dining room to his messy office. He tripped a latch and opened a hidden door.

"You have more secret passages?"

"Sort of." They passed down a central hallway and came out to the main hall once more. "This was used by the servants to access the first-floor rooms without being seen. There's a door to the dining room as well as the library, but that door is fixed closed now. There's another of these halls on the other side of the house as well."

"Does anyone use them anymore?"

"Just me. It's a way I can get around if I need to when there is a tour going on. Most of the time I can join one and no one is the wiser, but every now and then a guide will feel compelled to introduce me to the guests. They love it, and I will sign their maps and guides for them, but I like to just be able to live my life."

"I suppose." They came out in the hall, which was deserted once more. Randall led the way out the doors at the back of the hall and out into the end of the verge.

"Holy crackers," Sawyer said at the wide line of green with an abundance of flowers that stretched for nearly a hundred feet.

"Just walk down the path in the center and out along that way. If anyone approaches, just smile, wave, and keep going." Randall wasn't in the mood to play lord of the manner for tourists today.

A riot of color spread in front of them. His mother had redesigned these gardens when he was a boy. They had gotten overgrown and out of control, so his head gardener had asked if they still had the plans, and then did a complete restoration of his mother's garden. It made him feel close to her when he was out here.

Tourists holding brochures ambled along the paths, thankfully playing no attention to them. At the end, Randall continued across the lawn to a break in the hedge. He opened the gate and they passed through to a more "backstage" area.

"This is where I keep my horses," Randall said, pointing out an old stone shed that he had converted to the small stables. It wasn't fancy, but it kept the horses out of the weather and gave them a warm home. When they stepped inside, two heads perked out of their stalls. "This is Caesar and this is Augustus. They're both well-behaved geldings. In a day or so, once we've had a chance to rest, we'll go out riding and I can show you some of the sights on the estate you can only see from horseback." He smiled, and Sawyer strode over to him. Before Randall could react, he was engulfed in strong arms, deep blue eyes entranced him, and then Sawyer's musky scent threatened to buckle his knees…

and that was before he kissed him with such fervor that Randall was glad he was being held, or else he wasn't going to be able to find that damned floor. His heart raced, and Sawyer kissed him into near oblivion.

A throat clearing lifted the lustful haze around them and earned whoever was interrupting a glare. "Sorry, sir. I was coming in to check on the horses. Maybe I should go and come back later." Before Randall could stop him, the groom was gone.

"Who was that?" Sawyer growled.

"The groom. The man who cares for the horses. He lives in the village with his parents and stops in before and after school. I think you scared him away."

"Shit," Sawyer said under his breath before backing away and hurrying out. "Hey, come back. It's okay," Randall heard Sawyer say, and then he returned with Clive. "Randall says you care for his horses. They look in fine health, so you must be doing a really good job."

"I love the horses. His Lordship's are really beautiful, and someday I want to become a vet. But I have a long way to go." Clive was just eighteen, but Caesar and Augustus were like his best friends, and he cared for them as such.

"Then you do what I do. I care for the horses on a ranch in Wyoming. I train them too, and help with the cattle when it's needed."

"So you're a real cowboy," Clive said. "That's so cool." It seemed Sawyer had won over Clive.

"Randall and I have been traveling for what seems like forever, but tomorrow I thought we'd go for a ride. I'll leave a note when I do so you'll know."

Randall leaned against the door post, listening as Clive and Sawyer talked about horses. Every now and then Sawyer's gaze caught his and they shared a smile. Then Sawyer would continue whatever story he was telling.

"I should be going. Randall was just introducing me to the horses and showing me some of the area. But I'm sure I'll see you later. Maybe we can go riding sometime." Sawyer and Clive shared a fist bump, and then Sawyer joined Randall again, slipping an arm around his waist. "Thank you," he added softly.

"For what?"

Sawyer stopped, looking at him as though he were daft. "Trying to make me feel at home." He leaned closer. "Now, how about we go back to the private area of your freaking huge house and pick things up where we left off before Clive came in?" His eyes smoldered, and Randall once again found himself nodding and half floating on air as they returned to the house.

"JESUS," RANDALL whispered once he and Sawyer were in his bed. Holy hell, the man was voracious. Randall didn't know which way to turn, and it didn't matter. Sawyer was all incredible hands and exploring lips, pushing Randall onto a plane of ecstasy he never knew existed. *Eyecrossing* was the word that came to mind, and Sawyer showed no sign of stopping.

Covered in a sheen of sweat that glistened in the sunshine peeking through the windows, Sawyer was glorious, and the fact that he wore his hat only revved Randall up even more. It seemed he had found his kink, and fuck if it wasn't Sawyer, naked, skin glistening, muscles heaving, and that fucking cowboy hat still on his head.

Sawyer leaned over him, and Randall gasped with passion just before Sawyer kissed him hard, drawing Randall a little closer to heaven. This was sheer delight, and he was thankful no one could hear them and that the house was closed for the day, or else the tourists would be getting a bonus performance. Not that he wanted Sawyer to stop for any reason. He wanted this to go on forever, with Sawyer sending him flying to the moon and back as often as possible, which he did over the next half hour until Randall couldn't take it anymore and his control shattered as he held on to Sawyer to keep from flying to pieces.

Randall lay in the quiet of his bedroom, with only Sawyer's soft breathing and the sound of the rain, which had started again, dripping outside the window. It was still early evening, but the light of the day was fading fast because of the cloud cover.

"Drip, drip, drip," Sawyer said from next to him. "It took me a few seconds to realize what that sound was. We don't get this much rain in Wyoming except maybe in the winter, and then it's mostly snow. I'm glad that isn't falling or we'd freeze our bits off." He nestled closer. "I think we need something to eat. My stomach is starting to think my throat has been cut."

Randall sighed. "I can see what there is in the house, but there probably isn't a great deal. I…."

Sawyer shrugged. "Isn't there a restaurant or something? You said there's a village."

"There's the pub."

Sawyer jumped out of bed. "Then let's go there."

Randall paused and then shook his head. "I don't go there very often. My father was a staple there. It's where he did a lot of his drinking. So many of the men used to love him because he was the good-time earl and he would buy rounds of drinks, especially once he'd had a few."

Sawyer tugged him up and into his arms, holding him skin to skin. "You are your own man, and you don't have to act like your father or try to be him."

"I know that," Randall said more strongly than he intended.

"Come on. I'm hungry, and this pub seems like the perfect place to get something to eat. You can talk and reacquaint yourself with the people in the village, and you can also show them that you are different from your father. You don't need to buy a round or get drunk. Be you and let them see who that is." Sawyer held him so tightly, Randall actually thought anything was possible.

"Fine," he groaned. "Let's go to the pub." He wasn't sure what kind of reception he was going to receive.

CHAPTER 13

TO SAY the building looked old was an understatement. The place had been built centuries before, and was laden with heavy wooden beams and dark, scuffed, worn wooden seats that had seen centuries of butts. The inside seemed permeated with the scent of tobacco, even though no one was allowed to smoke inside any longer.

As he entered, Sawyer made sure to put on a smile. A few heads turned his way with curious looks, but the entire room went silent when Randall came in. Sawyer swore he could hear his boots on the floor every time he stepped.

"There's a table over there," Sawyer said, gesturing toward the empty seats. Randall continued looking around, standing in the center of the room as everyone seemed to lower their gaze.

"What can I get your Lordship?" the man behind the bar asked after a slight bend of his head.

"Randall," Sawyer said gently. "He and I will each have a beer, and what is your best dish?"

"Our shepherd's pie," the man answered.

"Then we'll each have one of those and the beer," Sawyer said. "Thank you." He didn't know what the protocol was at a moment like this, so he guided Randall to a seat. He took it, and eventually conversation in the room slowly began, only this time he was pretty sure all of it was about them.

"This was a bad idea," Randall said softly.

"No. This is a great idea. You need to be seen, and they need to know that you aren't some dragon in your castle or an ogre that is going to eat their children. You don't have to be their drinking buddy, but you and they are connected. If you want to succeed, then you have to help them be successful, and that takes talking. And maybe having a beer with them occasionally." The bartender brought their beers in pint glasses. Sawyer tasted his and licked his lips before downing a quarter of the glass.

"This is way better than the stuff at home. Though it should be colder," he whispered and drank some more. Then he looked for the bartender and caught his eye. "This is very good."

"You a Yank?" he asked.

"Yes. I'm an American." He took off his hat and placed it on his lap. He'd forgotten he had it on.

"One of them cowboys?" a man asked from behind him.

"You bet. I wrangle horses and herd cattle out in Wyoming. I'm here staying with Randall for a couple of weeks. I met him when he was visiting mutual friends." He refused to say *his Lordship* because that was not who Randall was to him. He was his boyfriend, and their relationship was personal and had nothing to do with social hierarchy. He turned to the man who had asked. "I spend most of my time outdoors, the way you do, judging by how windblown and suntanned your face is."

"And you're here with his Lordship?" He sounded shocked.

"Sure." Sawyer turned to sit forward in the seat. He kept his opinion to himself, but it was becoming clear that these people had no idea who Randall was or that he was a good guy. Sawyer drank some more of his beer, and when the food arrived, he dug in.

"Good?" he asked Randall, who nodded as he took a delicate bite.

"I haven't had one of these since I was a kid. One of my nannies used to have it made for me."

"If you like it, then tell the man. He looks like he's about to shit a brick," Sawyer said, and the man behind him chuckled. "Just treat these folks the way you did the people on the ranch. If they ask for your opinion, give it. If they do something good, praise them for it. If they need help, be there to provide it if you can. Everyone on the ranch worked together, because if they didn't, the entire place would fall apart." It was pretty simple to him, but then he wasn't Alan or Mrs. J, and his name certainly hadn't been on the sign at the entrance to the drive.

"You don't understand how things are here," Randall told him.

Sawyer shrugged. "It seems to me that things here are largely dictated by how you act. They will all follow your lead. So do that and be the one out front." He ate some more of the shepherd's pie.

"Is everything to your liking, your Lordship?" the bartender asked. He was probably the owner of the pub; he was doing everything but wringing his hands with worry.

"The pie is great. Reminds me of what I had as a child. Thank you," Randall said, and damned if the barkeep didn't give him a smile. "I've been away for a while, but it's good to have some home cooking again."

"Yes, this is wonderful," Sawyer agreed as he dug in to finish off the last of it. He also finished his beer but turned down another one. If he had a second, he was pretty sure the jet lag would catch up with him, and the last thing he wanted was to go to sleep too early. At least that was what the internet told him.

The man beamed and hurried back behind the bar to fill other orders.

"So, gentlemen, what's been happening in the village?" Randall asked, looking around. Again, no one said anything, maybe expecting it to be a trick question. "There has to be something interesting. I've been in America, and I got to work with some amazing horses. You always raised beauties," he said, turning to one of the older men. "How does this year's crop look?"

"Very good, your Lordship," he answered softly.

"Would it be all right if we stopped by to see them? Sawyer absolutely loves horses." Damn, Randall was really trying to break through, but these people were giving him nothing. Sawyer didn't understand why, but Randall didn't seem ruffled by it.

"You want to come see my horses?" Shock was plain on his face until he schooled it. "Of course. Stop by any time, your Lordship." He actually seemed pleased, and Sawyer began to wonder if he should order that second beer after all.

Randall met his gaze once again, and this time there was doubt in his eyes. Sawyer wasn't sure what the issue was, but he had a feeling it was something Randall needed to wrestle with himself and come up with his own answers. Sawyer could give him a start, but he couldn't dictate his actions. Though he was a man and dictating would be the easier solution… at least to his way of thinking. But he held back.

"I think it's time we dispense with this 'your Lordship' stuff. My name is Randall, okay? His Lordship was my father, and he's dead." Randall pulled himself straighter, but he didn't stand up like he was making a grand announcement. He stayed seated like he was just having a conversation. Sawyer wished he could do more to give him his support. "We all know that my father…."

"It's not right to speak ill of the dead," someone said, but probably out of habit rather than true feeling about his father.

Randall snorted. "We need to clear the air, so if I'm speaking ill about him, then he deserved it, and I certainly know that more than most of you. He was a bad father and an even worse landlord. He didn't do some of the things that he should have done. So I would like your help. I need to know what is lacking. If you rent from the estate, then what repairs need to be made? I will make a list so that it can be prioritized and the repairs and upgrades completed."

A murmur went through the group.

"Is he serious?" an older man with snow-white hair asked as he leaned over, propping himself on a cane as he did so.

"Yes." Sawyer nodded to reinforce the point.

"And if you or your children have building or handyman-type skills, please tell me about them as well. I want to make the repairs, and I want the money to stay in our community if at all possible." That got an even more of a murmur, people talking to each other with an undertone of excitement.

"Should we write to you?"

"How about you just email me?" Randall said and offered an email address. "That one comes right to me, not the staff at the estate. We need to work together to improve our community. This is long overdue, and I'm sorry for that." He went quiet and turned back to the table. He drank the last of his beer and closed his eyes.

"Do you want to leave?" Sawyer asked before motioning to the bartender. He asked about the bill.

"It's on the house," the bartender said.

Sawyer shook his head and leaned over the bar. "How about you let me pay for our food, and the next time someone comes up a little short, you take care of them instead?" He used the strange money to pay and thanked him once again for an amazing meal. They left the pub, and Sawyer looked around the small village with its mostly stone buildings. It was a little like stepping back in time. The streets were narrow, with the center of the town facing a small open square.

"I think that went well. At least I hope it did," Randall said. "With a lot of these people, there is so much history and tradition, and I don't know if I can fight it."

"They certainly can't. You're the landlord for a lot of them, so they might feel like they're at your mercy. So you have to be the one to make the first move, and you did that very well." Sawyer opened the car door and realized he was on the wrong side. He grumbled under his breath and went around before getting in. "I'm not sure if you're going to get flooded with requests or if it is going to be radio silence."

"I know. But I need to know the condition of things."

"Give them some time. The brave ones will contact you, and the others will wait to see what happens." Sawyer knew what it felt like to not have much of a voice for a long time. It became hard to believe that anyone would ever listen to you.

Randall nodded his agreement and started the engine on the small BMW before pulling out of the parking space.

The sun had set and fatigue began to set in. The huge house was lit from the inside but seemed foreboding as they pulled up. Randall parked, and they went inside and into the rooms he used. The rest of the place was locked up tight and closed up for the night.

"Does it seem strange to have part of your house not really open for you? Like it's off-limits or something? The domain of tourists?"

Randall shrugged. "I still have access to the rest of the house, and I'll show it to you in the next few days. But having it open is an agreement with the National Trust. We still have inheritance taxes here, and they are hefty, so when my father inherited the property, he negotiated a deal that as long as the home was open to the public for a certain amount of time each year, the tax bill would be deferred. Now there are two of them that were deferred, because I'd have to pay as well. Otherwise I'd probably have to sell the contents as well as the house itself to pay them, and where would that get anyone? The tenants would be thrown into chaos, and it would be a mess not just for me, but the entire community."

"So you're doing what you have to do," Sawyer said and Randall nodded slowly. They settled in Randall's sitting room and listened to the rain pelting the windows. Sawyer was tired and wondered what arrangements Randall had in mind for them. He yawned and checked the time. It was barely nine o'clock, but dark with fog close to the ground.

"Tomorrow I'll show you through the house," Randall told him, and Sawyer closed his eyes. It wasn't long before Randall guided him out of the seat, took his hand, and led him upstairs to bed.

Sawyer was all turned around. He had slept deeply and it was definitely morning, but his body wasn't ready to get up. Still, he got out of the bed, scratching his hip on his way to the bathroom. He took care of business and found Randall in the bedroom with two mugs of coffee. He handed him one, and Sawyer sipped, groaning in sheer appreciation.

"You are a god, you know that?"

"I try," Randall said. "And you're naked." Damn, Randall's gaze slid down him. Sawyer put his mug aside and began dressing. Once he was done, he finished his coffee and joined Randall in the sitting room, where a tray of meats and cheeses with more coffee was set on a table. He settled in a chair and ate while Randall worked on his phone.

"I got two emails from the tenants. One says that the plumbing in their cottage is really bad, and another says that their lights aren't working properly."

"What are you going to do?" Sawyer asked, but Randall was already on the phone. He arranged for a plumber and an electrician to pay visits to the cottages that day. Then he ate a little and jumped to his feet.

"When we're done here, I'll give you a tour of the house. This afternoon we need to go to the village. I want to be there when the tradesmen show up so that the village will know that I meant what I said in the pub. Do you want to go with me?"

"Sure. Then can we go for a ride?"

"I don't see why not," Randall agreed. Sawyer finished his coffee and the cheese and meat. Then Randall took the dishes to his small kitchen and left them in the sink, and they headed out to start the day.

SAWYER WAS more than a little overwhelmed as they wandered down the portrait gallery. Randall held his hand, and Sawyer leaned against him when they stood in front of Randall's portrait. "You can definitely tell that's you. That glint in your eyes is still there sometimes."

"Really?"

Sawyer turned to Randall. "Oh yes. I see it when you look at me sometimes, and it's always special." He leaned, closer and Randall kissed him. "Why did your father have the portrait painted when you were so young?"

He shrugged. "My father never explained much of anything. He just told me I had to stand for it. I remember hating every moment of the ordeal. And in the end, I don't like it."

"I do. I think it's pretty amazing." He drew closer. "It's a wonderful painting." He stepped back, and they continued on down the hall before entering a dining room set to receive royalty.

"Queen Victoria and Prince Albert stayed in the house for one night in the 1850s. This is a recreation of the table as it was set for their dinner. It's a bit of a miracle that the tablescapes weren't sold at some point, but they stayed intact. The dishes and the glassware are all the ones used at that dinner. You can see the glasses with VR inscribed on them are the ones actually used by the queen and the prince. Most of the furniture in here is original as well." He motioned to the next room.

"This is wonderful," Sawyer said as they moved into a delicately decorated room. "Is this for the women?"

"Yes. It's the ladies' parlor. After dinner, the women would come in here for conversation while the men would either stay in the dining room or retire to the library for port and cigars. My great-grandfather decreed that the men always stay in the dining room. He hated cigars and didn't want his books to smell like them. In fact, few people ever smoked at all here out of respect for him."

Every room was breathtaking. Sawyer couldn't imagine living this way, especially with so many rooms with a particular purpose. "I grew up in a house that was small enough to fit inside some of these rooms."

Randall sighed. "I didn't grow up in these rooms either. They were already being used for tourists when I was a boy. Though I loved to sneak into the rooms while the tours were going on, or I'd hide in the passageway and pop out behind people to scare them." He chuckled.

"You were naughty."

"I was a kid, and I lived in this huge building where most of it was off-limits." He led the way back to the great hall. "By far my favorite room in the house is the library. If I could, I'd take it off the tour so I could use it myself, but it's far too important." He opened the door, and Sawyer stepped into the room he'd seen the day before. "There are over ten thousand books in two levels of cases. There are also a number of additional books in the antelibrary, which is in my portion of the house. We have books that go back almost seven hundred years in this room. Again, it's a miracle that some of them weren't sold."

"Who is that?" Sawyer asked of the portrait above the fireplace.

"It's a period portrait of Queen Elizabeth I. The story is that a friend of the third earl needed some money, so he sold him the portrait. It's one of the most important pieces in the house. There was talk of it being sold some years ago, but thankfully it never happened."

"It must be interesting to have your entire family history laid out all in one place," Sawyer said. "I don't know much about my family. I knew my grandparents on my mother's side. They helped take care of me when I was young. But they died before I was six. I don't know if my father spoke to his parents. I don't remember ever meeting them, and there certainly aren't pictures of them lining a room somewhere. More like photographs in some long-forgotten attic." In a way, he was a little jealous of Randall. If nothing else, he knew where he came from. All Sawyer had was himself. Sawyer drew closer and began looking at the books in the cases.

"I've heard of some of these."

"Yeah. The sixth earl was a reader. He claimed to have read almost every book in this library. At least the ones that were here at that time. He also loved American books, so there are copies of some of your classics, like *Tom Sawyer* and *Walden.*"

"Excuse me," Celeste said quietly from the doorway. "The first tour will start in ten minutes."

Randall nodded. "Thank you. We'll be out of here before then."

She stepped into the room. "I wanted to ask you—would you be okay with adding an additional tour? We have sold out the next three days and are turning people away. It would only be for the next week or so. It's been very busy."

"That's fine. Of course. Go ahead, as long as you have people to lead it."

"Thank you," she said and left them alone.

"Do they always come to you with questions like that? Shouldn't they be able to make those kinds of decisions on their own?" Sawyer asked.

Randall shrugged. "I suppose they should, but there's a sort of bounty of riches. I could open the house to more tours, but then with that many people coming through, it wears on the house itself. Lots of people with their damp breath, heavy shoes, touchy hands. All of it affects the house. So we limit the number of tours and have limits on the number of people per tour. I don't want to impact the house too greatly, but...."

Sawyer nodded. "I get that." He expected to go through the hidden door to Randall's rooms, but Randall took him by the hand and led him out and up the main stairs to the second floor. "There have to be ways to generate a little extra money without impacting the house itself."

"There probably are, but I haven't...."

Sawyer squeezed his hand. "I wasn't criticizing, just thinking out loud. Not that I have any answers." They paused at the top of the stairs to peer down at the great hall before taking a right down the hallway to a room with an open door. "What's this?"

"The tour includes some of the bedrooms as well as a few of the servants' rooms on the third floor, but I thought you might like to see this. It's where Queen Victoria and Albert slept on their visit. We don't have pictures of what it looked like, but we do have the house records, so we set the room up to appear as it might have when they arrived." Randall drew closer, his scent nearly overwhelming, making Sawyer want to tug Randall down to the other end of the house, close the door to the room they were using, and take him. He shook his head to get control of himself.

"So a queen slept here." Sawyer snickered.

Randall rolled his eyes. "Anyway. Yes, she did. It was a huge deal at the time and helped propel the family into the upper echelons of society. There are records of how much it cost to host them, and let me say it was no bargain-basement visit. By all accounts the visit was a success, and the queen even wrote a thank-you note. It's in the case."

Voices gathered below, and they continued down the hall, where they peered into rooms and then continued on. Some were furnished while others were empty. "What do you do with all these?"

"I'm not sure. Most aren't on the tour, so we leave them empty. They get cleaned periodically, and every room is checked daily to ensure that there isn't an issue." They continued on and through a door at the end of the hall, and found themselves back outside Randall's bedroom. Sawyer did his best not to yawn, even though his body told him he should still be asleep.

"I think we should find something to do until your meetings in the village. It's either that or I'm going to go back to sleep. I'm all messed up."

"Then come on. How about we kill two birds with one stone? We can saddle up the horses and ride into the village, maybe have lunch in the pub, and we can meet the contractors afterwards."

Now that sounded amazing to Sawyer. He found his boots and pulled them on. Then he checked that he looked okay before following

Randall down and out the front door, to the delight of a group of tourists. Granted, Sawyer knew he was just part of the scenery. A few people asked Randall to sign their tour books, but a few of the girls asked him for selfies, and he obliged.

It took a while to get over to the horses and get them saddled. "These are different."

"They're English saddles. They sit a little differently, but I'm sure you'll get used to it pretty quickly." Randall finished checking everything over, and then they mounted up and took off across the estate. "Since we have time, I want to show you one of my favorite places."

CHAPTER 14

THE CLOUDS from the day before were gone and the sun shone brightly, illuminating the lush green that seemed to come from everywhere as Randall mounted Caesar. He loved watching Sawyer on a horse, and damn, he was as stunning as ever on Augustus. They headed out along the back drive, and then Randall pointed and they veered off across one of the great lawns laid out in the style of the Victorian period, the sun brightening the entire world. Sawyer gave his horse his head and seemed to fly over the ground.

Randall let him. It was a ways to his spot, and there was something freeing about just letting go. He didn't let his horse travel as fast, but that was fine. He loved watching Sawyer.

As they reached the far side of the lawns, Sawyer slowed, and Randall caught up before taking the lead on one of the forest paths. "This part of the estate was used for hunting. They used to shoot ducks and grouse out here as well as pheasants. There were fox hunts with packs of dogs and men in red jackets on horseback. It was all very civilized and a real ritual, though that kind of hunting isn't done any longer."

"Did you ever do it?"

"A couple of times, but we used a scent and had it dragged on the ground, so no foxes were actually hunted. Still, it was fun with all the dogs and people. I've never hunted here. That was at a neighboring estate, and it was for charity." They continued through the trees, which spread a thick canopy over them.

"This must be an old forest," Sawyer commented. "The trees are huge."

"Yes. This part of the estate has never been timbered. These trees are hundreds of years old. My grandfather actually leveraged this part of the estate with the tax people. He told them he could sell off these trees and have them cut to pay part of the debt, or they could help protect them. They gave in, and it was agreed that this section of land be left to nature." He continued on.

"Wow," Sawyer gasped as they broke out of the trees and into the hidden glen. Grasses and a small lake filled the space. "Is this natural?"

"Yes. There's a small creek that flows through the property, and it replenishes this little lake. Tons of animals come here to drink and feed. My father wanted to find a way to include this in the more manicured portion of the estate, but it didn't work out. So this is a little hidden gem."

"What sort of animals are back here?"

"All kinds." They sat on horseback together, and Sawyer took his hand. "If we're quiet, there will be ducks that land, and there are plenty of rabbits in the grasses. Squirrels fill the trees, and if we were to stay awhile, we might see larger animals, but they tend to come out at sunrise and sunset." He pointed. "Look over there. A family of foxes has a den in that copse of trees. Sometimes I've seen them playing with the little ones. This is my own private piece of England, the part of it that I love the most."

Sawyer squeezed his hand. "Do you ever go swimming? Or did you when you were a kid?"

Randall shook his head. "The stream is spring-fed, so it's cold all the time. We used to play in it when I was a kid sometimes, but I never swam. Sometimes I wish I'd had brothers to play with. Then things might have been different. But I didn't have lot of time for things like playing. I was watched over by nannies, and then when I was old enough, I was sent away to school."

"There had to be happy times." Sawyer leaned closer. "What about Christmas?"

"The house was always decorated for the holidays because the guests expected it. But our part was sparse. My father usually had a present for me, and my mother would have a few things, but it wasn't a big deal. I know my grandfather spent the holiday visiting in the village. He would bring small gifts to the tenants and have oranges and such for all the kids. I think my father spent the day getting pissed."

"Jesus. My father was no barrel of laughs, but he used to love the holidays. So we did a few things as a family. After Mom died, we spent the time with relatives, until he wore out his welcome in one way or another." Sawyer's phone chimed, and he pulled it out of his pocket. "Speak of the devil."

"It must be four in the morning in Wyoming."

Sawyer answered and put the call on speaker. "Where the fuck are you, boy? I tried calling and it went right to voicemail. I figured I would try the middle of the night and see if you answered. Where are you?"

"I'm out of the country," Sawyer said. "And that is all I'm going to tell you."

"I went by the ranch, and they said you were gone. That you had left." His voice held a frantic edge. "Where can I find you? I'm in trouble, and you need to help. You owe me, boy."

Sawyer grew agitated, and the horse began shifting his weight, picking up on Sawyer's unease. "That's enough. I don't owe you anything, and I'm thousands of miles away from you. I'm not paying any of your gambling debts. If you're in over your head, then get yourself some help. You really need it. But stay away from me." He pressed the red button to end the call. A few seconds later it rang again. "Block."

"Good for you. No one at the ranch is going to tell him where you are, and now he's cut off. He'll have to sink or swim on his own."

Sawyer sighed. "He'll sink. I don't think he has the strength to do anything else. But I can't let him sink me too. He's had a problem for a long time, and he doesn't know how to stop. My father won't get any help...."

"He keeps saying you owe him," Randall probed, trying to figure out what the hell that meant.

"Yeah. Like since his sperm is valuable or something," Sawyer said. "Or all the times I had to scrounge for something to eat was a life lesson." He rolled his eyes. "My father is a selfish asshole, and I hate that he's making me angry even though I'm way over here." He looked out over the lake and grew quiet. Over time he calmed down, but Randall knew this hurt him.

"Both our fathers should never have been parents," Randall pronounced, and Sawyer nodded slowly. "Somehow our job is to get past all that."

"Yeah." They sat together for a while, listening to the breeze rushing through the grass. "We should get to the village if we're going to have lunch before you meet the workmen."

"All right." He wasn't sure if Sawyer was looking for a change of subject or simply wanted to stop talking about this. "You know you don't need to be embarrassed or anything."

"Yeah... well... I guess I am, and I don't know how to handle it. My father is a compulsive gambler. He will take a bet anywhere and anytime. It's pretty bad." He lifted his head enough that Randall could see the trouble in Sawyer's eyes. "Why did we need to scrape the bottom of the barrel when it came to fathers? I bet Alan and Chip had a real good father. I know he died and left the ranch to the care of Mrs. J and Alan, and that they had a hard time of it for a while, but by all accounts he was a good man. Didn't we deserve fathers like that?"

Randall made no move to leave. "We get the luck of the draw when it comes to parents. If you ask me, every child deserves a father like that. It doesn't mean you get it, though." He cleared his throat. "Did you ever think about having kids? Do you want them?"

Sawyer hesitated, gazing away from him. "I don't know. What if I turn out like my father? No kid deserves that."

Randall couldn't help laughing softly. "Do you really think that? You are nothing like your dad. You're thoughtful and gentle. You care about other people and look after them. Sawyer, you're one hell of a man, and any kid would be lucky to have you as a parent." He cleared his throat. "I have to have a child. I need a son and he must be mine, or else the entire estate will go to some distant cousin or other, and I have no idea who that is."

"Do you have to marry the child's mother?" Sawyer asked very softly, his words carrying on the wind.

"No. As long as I acknowledge the son as mine, then that is enough. I was thinking about looking into surrogacy. I know that Alan and George are doing the same thing."

"Okay. I get that you need to have a son, but do you want one?" Sawyer asked. "There's a huge difference."

"I know. That's what I need to be sure of." He turned his horse and headed back down the trail, with Sawyer behind him. That was the big question, and one he didn't trust himself enough to answer.

LUNCH AT the pub was as good as dinner had been the night before. Sawyer seemed to think so too, judging by the speed at which he ate his bangers and mash. "On Fridays, we do fish and chips," the server told them with a smile. "It's my favorite."

"Good to know," Sawyer told her, returning the smile. "Randall and I will have to come in to see how it is one of these weekends."

She took their dishes and hurried away.

"How do you do that? You flash a smile and everyone goes all gooey-eyed."

"I'm just being nice, and they do not," Sawyer protested.

"Yes, they do. That server is barely legal, and she's looking over here dreaming about taking you for a ride." Part of him was teasing and part was jealous.

Sawyer glanced to the server and then back, his cheeks reddening. "I was just being nice. My mama told me that being nice to people didn't cost anything, and sometimes it came with plenty of rewards. It's not like I'm interested in her."

"I know that," Randall told him. "I guess I wish I had your charm, your way with people. They respond to you." What a huge change between the uncommunicative, almost grouchy man he had first met. Sawyer was certainly a bit of a mystery, but that was good. Randall was pretty sure Sawyer was never going to be boring.

Randall paid their bill when the server returned, and he thanked her before heading out. They mounted their horses and continued down the lane to the first house, where the plumber's van was already parked out front.

"Your Lordship," Steven Bishop said as he hurried out of the house with a huge grin. "I thank you for the help, but I wasn't expecting you." He was all flustered.

Randall climbed down from Caesar, and Sawyer dismounted as well, taking the reins for him. "I wanted to make sure that everything was being fixed and that you were being looked after."

"I am, thank you. The plumber is still working. He says some of the pipes need to be replaced, and he's doing that now."

Mrs. Bishop hurried out. "I'd offer you and your friend some tea, but I don't have any water." She seemed nervous.

"It's all right. You let me know when the plumber is done and if the problem is fixed. That's the most important thing." He shook hands with both of them and then climbed back on his horse. He smiled and waved before continuing through the village. He greeted most people he knew with a nod and another smile. If he stopped to speak with everyone, the electrician would have come and gone before he got there. In fact, he was putting his tools back in his van as they arrived.

Randall dismounted and strode up to the electrician. "Is everything okay?" he asked. "Were you able to fix the problem?"

"Partially. The wiring in there is really old. They have fuse boxes rather than a more modern wiring system. I was able to find the short, and that's been resolved, but the real answer to the problem is to switch out the fuse box with a modern breaker box. That would make their entire electrical system more stable." He narrowed his gaze. "Are you the landlord?"

"My lord," Charles Granger said as he hurried out. "Thank you for helping us. We were afraid to plug anything in in the kitchen."

"It's no more than you deserve. As I said in the pub, things need to change, and we need to make sure that our village in in good repair. I'm just glad I could help." Randall tilted his head toward the electrician. He then nodded to both of them and wished Charles a good day before thanking both of them and heading out.

"That made you feel good," Sawyer said. "Helping them, making sure their homes are in good shape and safe."

"Yes. I also know that the floodgates are going to open." Charles and Steven were certain to share over a beer at the pub that Randall had taken care of their issues, and the others who had hesitated to come forward definitely would now.

"But you'll know what their issues are and then you can fix them. If there hasn't been a lot of maintenance, you're going to have quite a few issues that have been neglected, and who knows what kind of structural issues."

"I know. The ones I had today were easy. What am I going to do when someone comes to me with something that means the cottage is too unsafe to live in?" His mind was already racing ahead to issues that hadn't even come up yet. "My father drank away a lot of what should have been put back into the village." They continued through town and out the other side, letting the horses plod along. "How am I going to afford all of this?"

"What you do is you need to assess all of the things that are reported, and the most critical or life-threatening are the ones that get fixed first," Sawyer said. "And I was thinking that maybe you can enlist the villagers to help. Come up with your list, analyze it, and maybe sponsor a village work day or something. Like a barn-raising back home, where folks help each other out."

Randall nodded. He wasn't sure that would work, but he knew he didn't know very much about building trades and managing a village.

His father had never told him much about what was expected of him. He suspected his father had done such a bad job with the property that he didn't want Randall looking over his shoulder. If it would bring in money, his father was all for it, but when it came to the responsibilities that he had to others, he really didn't care. And Randall could see that was wrong and that he and his family had stayed away and out of people's lives for way too long. "We'll have to see what people say."

"True," Sawyer told him. "But keep in mind that what they say probably isn't the whole truth. I'm not saying they're lying, but they could be reporting a symptom rather than the root of the problem. Like today. They said that they had a short and were afraid to use their kitchen outlets, but the real cause of the problem is that their electrical system is old, worn out, and needs to be replaced. That's going to cost quite a bit more than just a visit from the electrician you had today."

"I see. I don't know anything about this sort of thing."

"I do." Sawyer smiled. "I can fix just about anything. I used to help out Mrs. J all the time at the ranch. I can't rewire a house, but I know when things are wrong and enough to start to pinpoint the source of the problem. When people report things, we can review them together." Sawyer pulled to a stop. "Now, which way do we go? It seems like we're just wandering, and that's fine, but I have no idea where we are."

"This road winds around and ends up on the north side of the estate, so if we keep going this way, we'll be fine."

"Cool." Sawyer seemed content to ride along. A few cars came up on them from behind, but they slowed and often waved as they passed. This was the country, after all, and drivers were used to encountering horses from time to time. At the large oak tree, a local landmark, he made a right turn, and they started following a cross-country trail that Randall had taken many times before. He knew each tree and glen as they passed, following the creek bed for part of the way, before crossing and continuing on until the house loomed in the distance.

"God. Every time I see this place, it takes me by surprise. It's like a movie set."

"Sometimes I think it's a horror movie," Randall quipped.

"Do you really? Most people would envy you," Sawyer said, pulling to a stop. Randall did the same. "To most people, living in a place like this would be a dream. That's why so many people come to visit, you know. They want to live that fantasy, if only for a little while.

I mean, most people don't come to see fancy paintings, antique books, or the impressive rooms. They come to be part of it all, at least for a little while." Sawyer paused and gasped. "Have you ever thought about offering something different as a way to fulfill some of their fantasies?"

"Like what?"

"You Brits have tea, right? So while you're in residence here, offer tea with the earl once a week. You limit it to, say, twenty people, and then once a week, you sit down to tea."

Randall rolled his eyes. "And what would I have to do? Wear my official regalia?"

"No. You simply have tea with them, talk to them. Give the guests a taste of the fantasy they really long for. You'd eat with them, take a few pictures, and have a good time. That's all you'd need to do, and you could charge fifty bucks a person for it. It would be once a week, and you could schedule it in advance. You have a website for tickets and stuff, so you could add that too."

Randall sighed. "It's an idea." Truly, it was one that he hated. By and large he was an introverted person, and the thought of having tea with a bunch of strangers on a regular basis made his stomach flip.

"You don't like it," Sawyer said.

"If George did it, he would come shining through. I know he would. But why would anyone want to spend time with me? I may have a title, but otherwise I'm as dull as dirt. I'm not a good conversationalist, and I hate making small talk." He didn't want to think about why that was. "I'm terrible in social situations. My parents used to have dinners and entertain before my mother died. I would come down and make an appearance. I was never really invited to join them—I was too young, so I never became comfortable with that sort of thing around strangers."

"Okay. It was just an idea," Sawyer told him softly. "You shouldn't do things that you don't feel comfortable with."

Randall nodded. "But I appreciate the idea. I really do. Celeste keeps trying to come up with ideas to make the guest experience seem special, and I want that. We used to decorate the house for Christmas and have special tours, but it took such a toll on it that we stopped that a few years ago. Besides, every house does that. We close in late October, so in a week or so, and the house isn't open again for tours again until the spring." He stood, looking at his home.

"What do you feel when you look at it?" Sawyer asked.

Randall was taken aback. No one had ever asked him that before. "I don't know. I mean, it's my home, but there are parts of it that I feel disconnected from. The public rooms are part of the tour, so they don't feel like they're mine, even though they are. I think I feel most connected out here."

Sawyer nodded. "I can see that. Yeah, it's just a house—granted a big one—but it's a house. The land and being outdoors, that's something really special, and I suppose you feel the obligation to take care of it."

Randall swallowed hard. "I feel that more and more each day. Hell, I spent years trying to run away and hide from it. I let others take care of that part of the estate, and they did a good job, but I can see that doesn't mean I can walk away. The people in the village suffered because of my indifference." He pulled out his phone and chuckled. "And I'm just beginning to see how much. There are ten emails from people telling me about problems they are having. One has a roof that has been leaking for weeks."

"Okay, then. Let's make that the first priority. I can go over in the morning and take a look at it. I've fixed lots of roofs in my time, and if I can't fix it, I should be able to explain what's wrong and what needs to be done."

"You don't need to do that. Putting you to work isn't why I brought you here." Randall wanted to show Sawyer a good time in the hope that he might want to come back. The thought of him going home and Randall not seeing him again was getting harder to come to grips with. He knew that they should have parted ways before he returned to England, but with the issues with Sawyer's father, Randall had been able to use that as an opening for Sawyer to come here. But the underlying problem still remained. They would need to part, and then Randall would be heartbroken. It wasn't the first time, and it probably wouldn't be the last, but he had little doubt that their parting would hurt more than any other before.

"I need things to do. And if I can help, then I will." Sawyer leaned forward. "Come on, Augustus, let's show the English what we're made of." He urged his horse forward, giving Augustus his full head. Caesar didn't take much urging and he was off right behind, flying across the field as the house drew closer. Though Randall kept back a little ways, just so he could watch his cowboy in full action. There were few things more stunning, and Randall wanted to remember this for as long as he could.

As he got closer to the house, he veered off toward the stables, skirting the formal gardens and no doubt giving the guests milling about after their tour a full-on display of exactly what a cowboy could do on a horse. Randall followed in his wake, waving to the guests before taking the trail around the hedge to where he kept the horses.

"You gave them quite a show," Randall said, dismounting and pulling Sawyer into a hard kiss.

"Talk about a show," Sawyer growled before kissing him senseless in return.

Chapter 15

AN AMAZING week later, Randall was still next to him when Sawyer woke. They'd spent a lot of that week together in bed as well as exploring almost every section of the estate and the village. Sawyer had met a ton of people, and the last time he and Randall went to the village, folks stopped to speak to *him* as well as Randall. It was nice, and almost made him feel like he might belong here. Not that Sawyer had any illusions about who he was and where he belonged.

He slipped out from under the covers and spent a few seconds watching Randall sleep. It seemed like the only time when he wasn't worried about something, his face relaxed, without the lines around his mouth and eyes. Sawyer leaned over the bed and gently kissed him before going to the bathroom, where he used the facilities, dressed, and then left their rooms. He took the stairs to the main floor before going right outside.

It was still early, and more than anything, he wanted to go for a ride the way he and Randall had a few mornings, but he was on a mission of sorts, and he strode into the village and headed right for the pub, hoping they served breakfast.

They did, and he ordered something called a fry-up. What he got was an interesting combination of items, including beans, which he wolfed down.

"I take it you liked the food."

"Are you kidding? It was a cowboy breakfast with tomato." He grinned and finished his coffee before making inquiries about where he could find some of the people on Randall's list. Then he paid the bill and thanked the proprietor before heading off to knock on the first door, where they had a leaky roof.

"Morning," he said when they answered. "I'm Sawyer, and I wanted to look at your roof, if I may." He offered his hand, and the man shook it warily.

"Travis Manners." The man, in his late sixties or so, seemed shocked. "You're his Lordship's friend."

"Yes, and I have experience with roofs and such, so I thought I'd come by and try to help. Show me where it's leaking, and I'll take a look for you."

The man nodded and showed him inside, through the neat-as-a-pin house and back to the kitchen, where a room had been added on many decades earlier.

"I see. It's probably where the addition and the main roof meet. Is it okay if I go up and have a look?"

"I have a ladder," Travis told him. He took Sawyer out to what he called the back garden, where he showed Sawyer the ladder and then watched as he raised it to the roof and climbed up. The issue was not hard to spot. The roof was slate, something he had never seen before, but the principle was the same, and he spotted the issue pretty quickly before getting back down.

"The slates have shifted, probably in a storm with high wind, and they're letting some water in. I should be able to take up three or four of them and relay them again. Once I finish, the hole should be gone and the leak should stop. With this type of roof, I don't want to do anything more than I have to. It's been up there for many years, and the less fiddling done, the better."

"Oh, thank you. I'd get up there and try to fix it myself, but me leg doesn't work like it used to."

Sawyer smiled. "It's no problem. Is there a hardware store in the village?" He wasn't sure where to buy the supplies.

"No, but Carey's sells a little of everything. They might have what yer looking for." He pointed, and Sawyer hurried off in that direction. He entered the old store, and after what the man behind the counter called a good rummage, he found what he needed.

"You're the earl's friend," the man said, his gaze narrowing. "Don't know if I like the thought of you and him."

Sawyer shrugged. "Then don't think about it."

"You fixing something?"

"Mr. Manners's roof," Sawyer said warily. "He sent a note to Randall, and I was up early this morning, so I thought I'd help out." He paid and took what he'd purchased before hurrying back to the Manners cottage and climbing the ladder. It didn't take him but a few minutes to gently remove the slates and put them back into their proper place, sliding them under the ones above. He used a little adhesive to make sure they stayed and then surveyed his handiwork. It looked good, and he climbed down.

"There you are. It should be fixed, but you let me know after the next rain if it leaks again. Okay?" He doffed his hat with a smile. "I also put the ladder back where you had it."

Travis shook his hand and was all smiles. "Thank you. I was going to have to go up there, and Martha—she's visiting her sister in Manchester for a few days—she gets mad if I do things like that. Can I get you a cup of tea?"

"That would be nice," Sawyer said and sat at the kitchen table while he made the tea. He drank a cup, and after getting his ear talked off as he did, Sawyer said goodbye and gathered the leftover materials before heading to the next place on his list.

"HEY, COWBOY, you need a lift?" Randall said with the window down. "I hear you've been making the rounds already this morning."

Sawyer got in and pulled the door closed.

"I fixed the Manners's roof and stopped a flood in the Cooks' kitchen. These people take great pride in their homes, but they are in need of a lot of work. And it isn't just repairs. You need to make a full assessment of all the real estate you own and then, year by year, renovate these properties. I know a lot of them are historic and all, but they need new roofs, new plumbing and electrical. I'd say do three or four a year. It will take some time, but these systems are coming to the end of their lives, and they need a lot of work." Sawyer had done some patches, but more systemic changes were needed to take care of the root of the issues.

"That's sort of what I figured. If my father didn't help them out, that means they've been limping along for a lot longer than they should have."

"Okay. Then put together a plan to make the changes that need to be made."

Randall nodded. "I can see that's what I'll have to figure out." He pulled off to the side of the road. "Did you get something to eat?"

"At the pub, yeah. These are really nice people. But there is one thing. I think I had too many cups of tea. Everyone I talked with offered me one, and I didn't know how to turn them down."

Randall laughed. "Okay, I get that. It's the British thing to do. If someone comes to your door, you offer tea. If they help you out, you offer tea. If you inquire about their health and they want to chat, they offer tea. It's their way of being friendly. I have had more cups of tea in my lifetime than you can imagine. And I've found that the only way to say no is to have something pressing that you have to get to. Don't be specific, but gentle and caring, but you have a previous engagement that you must attend."

"I see. Though I suppose that will work for you. Everyone around here seems to think that you're very busy and have a lot of things to see to. I'm just a cowboy, so that really isn't going to work." If he stayed here for any length of time, he was going to have to get used to drinking a lot of tea. That was all there was to it.

"Your Lordship," someone called from behind them. Sawyer turned and got out of the car as Randall did the same. The man huffed as he caught up with them. "I'm sorry to disturb you."

"Mr. Cook. Is everything okay? Did the kitchen flood again?" Sawyer certainly hoped not. He'd spent enough time crawling around on their kitchen floor already, and he could have sworn he'd found the issue.

"No. It's good. Thank you." He took a few more deep breaths and then pressed a plate into Sawyer's hands. "Mrs. Cook just took some ginger scones out of the oven, and she asked me to bring them to you."

"Are these for me?" Sawyer asked. He inhaled and groaned. "You tell Mrs. Cook that they smell amazing, and that I will share them with Randall if he asks nicely. Otherwise I'll eat them all myself. Do you need a ride back home?" Mr. Cook really seemed stressed.

He seemed completely shocked, his eyes wide. "No. I don't want to put his Lordship out, but we wanted to say thank you for all your help." He turned and walked back more slowly down the road.

"We should go," Randall said.

Sawyer shook his head. "Give it a minute. Laticia told me that he smokes more than he should and has a touch of COPD. I just want to make sure he gets back okay." Sawyer took a bite of scone and passed one to Randall. "You know, if you ever decide to go with that 'tea with an earl' idea, you need her to make the scones for it."

Randall scoffed and then covered his mouth with his hand. Once he finished the scone, they got back in the car.

"WHAT IS this?" Sawyer asked as they pulled into a parking lot. Randall called it a car park.

"This is what used to be the stables," Randall told him.

Sawyer whistled. "You have to be kidding me. The horses lived in fancier accommodations than the people in the village." The building was brick with beams, and even the old stable doors were fancy and well built. Heck, the thing even had a clock tower.

"It was built at the height of the Victorian era when the country was booming, there was no income tax, and estates like this made money hand over fist. If you owned the land at that time, it was a license to print money. You controlled the food, the access to the woods, you got rent from the villages where many of the people who worked for you lived, and on top of that, the farmers paid you rent to farm your land. So in addition to all the fine art and furnishings in the house, the estate had some of the finest horses in this area of the country."

"Is that the gift shop?" Sawyer asked, pointing to where people were going inside.

"Yes. And the ticket office. This building also houses some of the management offices. We can go inside later, but this end has something I want to show you." He led the way down the long row of what had once been stalls and unlocked a door toward the end.

"People are watching you and pointing," Sawyer whispered.

Randall sighed. "It happens all the time. I can't go anywhere on my own land without someone seeing me. It's like living in a fishbowl a lot of the time." He pulled open the door and stepped inside. Sawyer followed him and closed the door before latching it closed.

"Oh my god," Sawyer whispered. "Is that a coach?"

"Yes. I've been working on it for a few years in my spare time. I found it, this carriage, and this buggy where the horses are now. I moved them into this section of the old stables. The store managers would like to expand, and they have their eye on this part of the building. I've been thinking of fixing up the estate manager's house and moving the offices there to give them extra room, but I don't want to give up this space."

"No," Sawyer agreed. "It's still really rough, and this is a workspace." He carefully opened the door to the coach and peered inside. The seats were lush and heavily padded. "Is that the same crest as on the glasses in the dining room?"

"Yes. The queen, after her visit, sent this to my ancestor as a thank-you for showing her such amazing hospitality. It even has her crest on the door. I want to finish it and the others and open this as a carriage display. I think that would be really fun."

Sawyer was already shaking his head. "Screw that. Finish this one and show it off, but the others, use them. Get the horses you need and use them on the property. God, I would love to drive a team of horses." He grinned as he ran his hands over some of the smooth wood. "Can you imagine taking a ride in this on a summer afternoon, or adding bells to the horses and using them at Christmas?" It was mind-blowing. "I wouldn't want to try to drive this one. It's too fancy and way too valuable, given its history, but the others?" He could just see riding in them. It would be like a dream come true. "A ride in any of them would be amazing." Every nook and cranny of this place seemed to harbor something special. He peered inside the coach and then walked all around it.

"Do you know what you're looking for?"

Sawyer laughed. "Not really. It just is really amazing. You've done a really good job with it."

"The thing was in pieces when I found it. The seats had been pulled out, and I found them in the attic of the house. They had been put away in storage. The wheels had been taken off, and the whole coach sat on the ground. It took a while to get everything back together. The biggest issue I had was with the suspension, but I managed to fix that too. The last thing I need to do is replace the hitching system. The wood is too weak to actually use, so I need to fabricate new parts."

"Where do you do that?" Sawyer asked.

"I have a small shop through that door." Randall opened it, and Sawyer peered in. All the tools were almost as old as the coach.

"You make everything by hand?" Sawyer asked, very impressed. He had no idea. "How did I not know this?" Randall had been able to help him with a lot of things, but he'd never let on that he knew how to create such beautiful things with his hands.

"I just use the old parts as a model and create new ones. I have a few modern tools over on the bench, because they save a lot of time, but I do all the final finishing with the hand tools. I really want the coach to appear as it did when it was gifted to the family."

Sawyer could understand that. "And the others?"

"They are going to take more work. A lot of the wood has rotted out in places and will need to be replaced. On the carriage, I'm going to need to have new wheels made. What's there isn't strong enough for actual use, even if they are in one piece."

"I've never made carriage wheels," Sawyer said. "I've made lot of other things. At the ranch we have to fix a lot of things, and sometimes that means making specific parts. The old stable needs a lot of care, and the horses take a toll on the wooden stalls, so I repair them all the time." But this was something completely different.

"This is close to making furniture," Randall said. "I know it sounds kind of dumb, but it is. These coaches and carriages were the chief mode of transportation in the day. This is what they had until the trains were developed. Can you imagine an entire network of horse-drawn conveyances all over the country? That's what we had. Then the trains came along, and that began to change. Later, the car pretty much did this sort of thing in."

"I think this is pretty amazing," Sawyer said. "And I really like that you're doing it yourself."

A pounding on the door made both of them jump. Randall growled as he hurried over, yanking it open with a glare. "This is off-limits. I suggest you rejoin your tour and stay with your guide." He didn't yell, but he was very clearly unhappy. He waited about two seconds before closing and latching the door once more. Sawyer joined him as Randall opened the door partway when the knock sounded again. "What didn't—?"

"I'm here to speak with Sawyer Kincaid," the man said with an eastern US accent.

Shit. All he could think about was that this was another of those damned people trying to collect on his father's debts. "What do you want? This is an area that is off the tour. It's a private area of the estate."

"I'm not here for the tour, though I'm sure it's very nice." He smiled, leaving Sawyer very confused. "My name is Arthur Wilson."

"Then why are you here? If this has anything to do with my father, I'm not paying his debts, and if you're here to make more threats, they aren't going to do you any good. I'm not paying for him. We put the last person who came to collect in jail, and I'm sure we can arrange to do that again."

The man stepped back, and Sawyer had to admit he did not look like any sort of debt collector. An accountant maybe or an attorney, but not a bruiser. He cleared his throat. "It seems your father has disappeared."

Sawyer shrugged. "Okay?" What else was he supposed to say? It was likely that the people his father owed money to had finally caught up with him. Either that or his father had managed to evade them and had somehow covered his tracks well enough that no one could follow him. "What does that have to do with me?"

"Well…." He cleared his throat again. "Do you really want to talk out here?"

"How did you find out where we were?" Sawyer asked. "I've been all over the estate and into the village today."

The man blushed. "I asked around. It wasn't hard to find a cowboy here in coastal England. I mean, no one else wears a hat like yours. I talked to a few people, and they pointed me to the estate. I just happened to be arriving when I was directed over here."

"Fine. Let's close up here and we can go up to the house so you can talk." Randall closed the door, and they headed back to the car. The man got into his own and followed them around to the side of the house. Then Randall invited him into his sitting room. "I'll leave you alone."

"No." Sawyer had no idea what was going on, but he had every intention of telling Randall what went on. This would save him the trouble. "Stay here."

Randall sat next to him.

"Can I get you some tea?" Randall asked, and Sawyer snickered.

"No, thank you. I've never gotten used to it. Anyway, I'm an attorney for your father's older brother. It would be your Uncle Dale."

"I have an uncle?" Sawyer asked. "I've never heard of him." He didn't know he had any family on his father's side. He knew he had cousins of some sort that were related to his mother, but he hadn't seen any of them in many years. Not since before she passed away. After that, it seemed they didn't want anything to do with him and his father. Though maybe that had more to do with his dad than him.

"I doubt you would have. Apparently Dale and your father hadn't spoken in years. I don't know the details of why. But Dale passed away, and from what is in the will, it seems it had something to do with your father's gambling. I believe that there was some sort of incident in the past. Anyway, your uncle passed away about two months ago, and your father and you are his only family. So I was asked to locate him and you. But judging by the stipulations in your uncle's will, your father doesn't qualify any longer."

"I don't understand," Sawyer said softly.

"Your uncle left a sizable estate. He was a financial advisor in Dallas and very successful. He left quite a bit of money, but there was a stipulation in the will that as long as your father was still gambling, he was not to inherit anything. Your uncle named you as his secondary beneficiary, with the same stipulation."

"Sawyer doesn't gamble," Randall said flatly, "and we know for a fact that his father is still gambling because people have been after him to collect on his debts. That's part of why Sawyer is here. We thought he would be safer if he was out of the country."

"All right. I'm going to need statements on what both of you know about your father's gambling and who he owes money to." He seemed a little overwhelmed. "I was hoping you might know where your father is."

"Nope. The last time I saw him, he was threatening me to try to get money so he could pay his debts. That was about ten days ago, I guess. He called to threaten me over the phone because he didn't know where I was. I think I got that call last week. I haven't heard from him since." Sawyer didn't know what to make of this, and he was grateful Randall was there with him.

"So as long as Sawyer's father is gambling, he doesn't inherit?" Randall asked.

"No. That isn't exactly true. If he stops gambling, then it doesn't change the will. It's written so that if your father hasn't already gotten help and is still gambling, which it seems he is, then he is permanently ineligible to inherit. All indications we've received in our inquiries indicate that he does not meet those qualifications. And that is the reason for my visit. I went to the ranch where you worked in Wyoming and had a devil of a time getting them to tell me where you were. I practically had to swear in blood that I wouldn't reveal where you were to anyone." He shivered.

"Mrs. J can be quite fearsome."

Arthur nodded. "And her husband was intimidating too. He made me sign a nondisclosure agreement. Those people are determined to keep you safe, that's for sure. You're obviously well liked and cared for. I asked them not to contact you because I needed to verify your father's situation before I contacted you."

"Thank you." Sawyer cleared his throat nervously. "So what else do I need to do?"

"Nothing at the moment. Now that I have found you, I need a permanent address and a way to contact you. Then I can submit the estate for probate. Once that's completed, the funds will be released to you. Under normal circumstances, this sort of thing takes a few months, but it could take longer given the complexity of the stipulations and the fact that your father could fight the will. We have no idea since we have been unable to locate him."

"While you were in Wyoming, did you happen to speak to the debt collector they have in jail who was threatening Sawyer for his father's gambling losses?"

Arthur nodded. "I believe we have a very good picture of what has been happening. But I must caution you. If and when you do receive the funds, they are not to be used in any way to pay for your father's debts. Your uncle stipulated that he and the rest of the family had been through enough trouble because of his gambling and that under no circumstances was any of his money to be used for that purpose." He seemed to relax a little now that he had delivered his message.

"That's no problem. I suffered enough too because of his issues. I'm not going to pay for them now." Sawyer pushed away the number of times his father had gambled away the food money or the rent and how many times they snuck out of town or were simply evicted and had to move somewhere else. "My father did not provide a warm, happy childhood. He seemed to become obsessed with making it big quickly. The next big score or some jackpot was just around the corner. There were days when the only time I got to eat was at school. So if anything comes my way, I'll abide by my uncle's wishes and not give my father a dime." The money was nice and all, but he wished he had known about his uncle when he'd needed him so badly as a teenager.

"Okay. Let me make a few notes." Arthur pulled open his case and a legal pad, writing things down as Sawyer waited. He asked a number of questions, which Sawyer answered, giving him his phone number and an email address. "Excellent. I'll forward you some forms that I'll need you to review and sign. Then we wait for approval."

"Thank you," Sawyer said, and they all stood. He shook hands with Arthur, and Randall did as well before showing him to the door.

"I don't think I've ever met an earl before," Arthur said softly at the door.

"You need to come to Wyoming. We have earls, dukes, and viscounts. Apparently we're the new hangout for the nobility." Sawyer grinned and thanked Arthur once more before closing the door.

"I take it that was completely unexpected," Randall said.

"I didn't even know I had an uncle. My father never mentioned him, and if I met him, it was when I was a baby. It seems kind of strange to have relations I didn't know." Randall snickered and pulled a copy of a thick book off one of the shelves. "What's that?"

"*Debrett's.* It's the definitive guide to the English peerage. It has all the family lineages, how we're related, and how titles were acquired and so on. Basically here, there are no unknown relatives unless some family is trying to harbor a real secret. And let me tell you, that's pretty rare and difficult to do." He opened the book to his family. "Here is a history of my family detailed from the first earl and how he was given the title and estate, and it goes through each successive generation." He pointed. "And here I am. The latest in a long line."

"I see. So you'd use that book to figure out who would inherit everything if you don't have children."

"Exactly. But because of how far back I'd have to go to find another relative, I'd probably get a lawyer and have him do the appropriate research for me. That way it would be done correctly. Though as I said before, I probably will have children of my own someday. I'd love to get married, and then I could find a surrogate to have an heir for me." He closed the book. "You really had no idea you had an uncle?"

Sawyer shook his head. "I know it sounds crazy. It does to me. I mean, some long-lost uncle dies and leaves me money? It seems like something out of a bad novel, and yet it happened. Granted, I don't know how much is involved or if I'm going to get anything at all, so I'm not going to count my chickens." He had plenty to deal with, and wondering about the *how muches* and the *whens* would only make his head spin. Arthur didn't seem too forthcoming in that department either, so maybe he wasn't authorized to divulge that information. Not that it mattered. "We should figure something out for lunch."

"The pub is always an option."

"Or one of us could cook."

Randall laughed. "Do you really think I can cook anything? No one taught me anything in the kitchen. I can do the most basic things and heat stuff up, but that's all."

"Me too. I'm not helpless, but I can't do anything fancy. So maybe the pub isn't a bad idea. The cooking there is a lot better than mine."

"Maybe. But what are we going to do? We can't eat at the pub all the time. If we do, there will be talk in the village. Though I suppose there is plenty of that already with the way we are with each other."

"Yeah, I'm sure you're right."

"Maybe I can talk to Celeste and see if she has any ideas. My mother used to have someone who came in and did the cooking. I usually eat at the club when I'm in London."

"That would have to be possible, and I'm sure there are plenty of ladies in the village who would be happy to come in and help you."

Randall sighed. "Yes. But I have to find one who isn't going to splash my business all over town." That was always the problem: people talked. "In a small community like this, not all that much happens, and I'm a private person. I don't want to be the subject of gossip, and I want to be able to lead the life I want...." He drew Sawyer to him. "I want to have a life with the people I care about, and I want that life to be ours. Yours and mine. Not the town's or anyone else's."

"Then you need to make it that way."

"No, *we* need to do that. It needs to be something you and I figure out."

And just like that, Sawyer's heart raced and he felt warm all over. He wondered if Randall could be serious. They had known each other less than a month, and yet Sawyer had never felt so at ease and so settled in his own skin. Yet he still wondered if this was something that was going to last. God, he hoped it did.

Chapter 16

Shit, maybe he'd made too much of a leap and he should have kept quiet and tried to beat around the bush some more in order to prepare Sawyer for what he'd been thinking.

"You want me to stay here?"

"Yes, I do."

Sawyer seemed speechless. "But what will I do? All I know is ranch work, and I can't do any of that here. You have two horses, and the farmers on your land manage all your livestock. What am I supposed to do, sit around and watch them? I can't do that. I have to keep myself busy, and the ranch is my home."

Randall nodded. He should have known this was a lot more to ask and needed more planning than just bringing up the idea and hoping Sawyer would fall in love with it in an instant. He had a life back in Wyoming, and Randall was asking him to give it up and move here to be with him. Hell, he really was as self-centered as his father. "There are lots of things you can do."

"Yeah, but all of them involve me staying here and leaving the ranch."

Randall lowered his gaze. "I know that. But I can't leave this place. I'm just starting to gain these people's trust, and I have so much work to do here. There are a ton of plans to make for how to manage the village and make things right with the people who rent from me. And it's not only what I'm going to do with the cottages, but I have to work out how to pay for all of it." That kept him up at night. "This house is going to need a new roof, and…." Randall felt the weight he'd tried for years to run away from slip fully onto his shoulders, and it wasn't going anywhere. "I can't do it alone."

"So you want me to stay and do it for you?" Sawyer asked. He didn't seem angry, but his voice was tinged with hurt.

"No. I don't want anyone to do it for me. I was hoping you'd stay and do it *with* me. I know I can't run away from this anymore. I have to stay here and be responsible for my family legacy. For years, I used the trappings that came with all this to try to escape. I spent most of my time in London and let the people I hired manage things here, and they've done a great job. But they aren't me. And while they can corral tourists and make sure the operations run smoothly, they can't ensure that I do right by the people who live on my land. Only I can do that." He sighed.

"Is that why you came to Wyoming? So you could find someone the way George had?"

Randall shook his head. "I didn't want to come at all. You remember—I was a complete asshole. I didn't want to be there. All I wanted to do was stay in my own little fantasy bubble and have things the way I wanted them. But I lost a bet to Alan, and then a certain cowboy with the brightest eyes and an attitude as tough as my own made me look at things differently. He didn't take any of my crap and had me mucking out stalls." Randall couldn't help smiling. "I bet if you shared that story in the pub, you wouldn't ever have to buy yourself another beer ever again."

"And you want me to stay?"

Randall scooted closer to Sawyer. "Losing that bet was the best thing that ever happened to me. It forced me to look at my life and the person I'd become. I was a real shitheel, and now I think I can see where I should be. And who I want to be here with me. Sawyer, I don't want you here to do what I should have done. I can get the work in the village completed. I can figure out the money and how to raise more of it. I know I can do all that if I have to. I'd figure it all out eventually. What I want is you here with me. That I know. I never saw myself here. This place, these rooms… they never felt like home to me."

"Do they now?" Sawyer asked, and Randall shrugged as he looked around.

"You feel like home to me." And just like that, everything in Randall's mind, all the years of searching and wondering if he would ever fit in anywhere, just settled right into place. He had the answer, and it was right here in front of him.

"I do?"

"I've lived part of my life in this house and on this land. There are places here that I love, but none of it felt like it was truly mine—and it really isn't. I'm just a caretaker of this estate, someone tasked with seeing it on to the next generation."

"But it is yours," Sawyer told him. "All of this, every painting and each and every stone, belongs to you, and this is your home."

"Everything may belong to me, as you say, but none of it feels like a home." He swallowed hard and tried to get Sawyer to understand how he felt. "If you and I were to go to London and stay there, then as long as you were with me, I'd feel like I was home." Randall leaned forward, his gaze locking on Sawyer's. "The ranch in Wyoming felt more like a home than I ever felt here, and I know now it was because you were there. It doesn't matter where we live. I feel at home… with you." He moved closer. "But I suppose the question I have to ask is if you think you could feel at home with me?"

Sawyer smiled. "I guess I could get used to living in a mansion and on an estate, but what am I going to do? I can't just stay here and do nothing, and I'm a guest here. It isn't like I can stay here forever. I'm assuming there are a bunch of laws about that sort of thing."

"There are, but all of that can be figured out. What I think is more important to ask is… what do you want to do? This is a big estate. Alan manages the livestock for George, and he sees to the land on his estate. In a way, he acts as the estate steward."

"I don't want to do that. Alan was always really good at managing the ranch. That isn't my skill."

"Then why don't you oversee the repairs and upgrades that need to be made? It's a big job, and you know a lot about making repairs and fixing things."

"I don't want to be the estate handyman," Sawyer told him, and Randall agreed.

"No, I don't want you making the repairs. Like you said, we're going to need to renovate the cottages a few at a time. I need someone who can prioritize what needs to be done and manage the repairs and upgrades. You'll be amazing at that, and the people in the village already like you." Randall slipped his hand under Sawyer's shirt. "I more than like you." He kissed him, pressing Sawyer back in the chair. "Will you at least think about it? I'm hearing from villagers almost every day. There's a lot to be done."

Sawyer growled and pulled Randall to him, deepening the kiss. "I'll think about it as long as you consider my 'tea with an earl' idea to help pay for it. We're going to need money to make all this happen."

Randall rolled his eyes. "Fine. I'll think about it. But it seems kind of tacky, and who is going to want to spend money just to have tea with me? Really."

Sawyer snorted. "I don't know, but we'll see. Maybe Mrs. Cook would like to run it for us. I can see." He was so excited. "We can serve those little cucumber sandwiches and give them so much tea, they float out of here."

Randall snickered. "You're having way too much fun with this." He glowered slightly. "You know that if I have to attend these teas, you will too." Sawyer growled. "I mean it."

"We'll see." He kissed him once more, and it seemed that at least for a while, the conversation portion of the afternoon was over.

Chapter 17

"Do you think you could help me?" a man asked as Sawyer rode one of the trails around the edge of the village. He pulled to a stop and dismounted.

"I can try." He was becoming used to folks stopping to talk to him. Word had gotten around that he had made repairs in the village, and a lot of people now asked for his advice.

"I don't want to bother his Lordship." Sawyer was quickly realizing that was their code for the fact that Randall still intimidated a lot of the people in the village, but they felt they could approach Sawyer. "But we are having troubles. The windows in our cottage don't always close well, so it can get cold in the winter, and the wind will blow in if it comes just right."

"How close by do you live?"

"Number 10, just up there," he said, pointing.

Sawyer nodded. "Okay. Give me a few minutes and I'll stop in to have a look." Great, he was going to end up drinking a ton more tea. It was the villagers' way of being polite, but he really wished they served coffee. Still, he climbed back on Augustus and rode slowly into the village, paying close attention to traffic. At number 10, he hitched the horse to one of the fence posts, which seemed sturdy enough. There was plenty of grass for him to eat.

The front door opened and the man stepped out. "Charles Whinton," he said.

"I'm—"

"We all know who you are, Mr. Kincaid," he said, shaking his hand. "And thank you for coming. My wife has rheumatism pretty badly, and the cold and damp aren't good for her."

"How long have you lived here?" Sawyer asked as he followed Charles inside.

"Oh, almost fifty years one way or another. I grew up in this cottage, and when my mum was ill, we returned to help her, and after I got a job here in the village, we stayed." He led Sawyer to the kitchen, where the windows had developed gaps.

"The frames seem sturdy enough," Sawyer said as he checked around and then stepped back. "The window frame is fine, but the sill under the window has gone soft, probably from years of cooking and dishes." He checked the other areas around the window. They seemed solid and dry. "Let me see where I can find a new sill. What I'll need to do is take out the old window, put in the new sill, and then size it before putting the window back in. That ought to fix it, and it shouldn't take too long."

"Oh, thank you. It will be nice this winter not having to worry about the cold air." He seemed relieved.

"It's no problem. Let me see what I can do, and I'll stop in to let you know." He paused before leaving the cottage. "You know you can talk to Randall about your issues."

"His Lordship…."

"Is a real good man, and he cares about the village and everyone in it. I know he's been gone a lot, but that's going to change. And he's no more important than you or your wife. Maybe it's the American in me, but everyone is equal. If the earl is your landlord, then he owes you the maintenance of your cottage, just as surely as you owe him the rent. I'm happy to help, but Randall will help you as well."

Charles seemed shocked. "I can't go directly to his Lordship. That's just… it almost doesn't feel right."

"I'm starting to understand that, but Randall is a good person and he wants to help." Sawyer smiled and then left the cottage and got back on Augustus before heading back toward the estate. They made their way back around the village on the back trail. All the people they passed waved, and Sawyer tipped his hat before heading off into the woods.

"Where have you been?" Randall asked warmly as soon as Sawyer approached the stable.

"I rode to the village and got corralled. Charles at number 10 is having trouble with one of his windows. The sill is gone and it's letting air inside. Is there an issue?"

"I don't think so. Arthur said he tried calling you, but he didn't get an answer, so he contacted the office. He wants to come out tomorrow to speak with you before he returns to the States."

"I'll call him and set it up after I rub Augustus down. I also need to find something to use to make a new windowsill." He walked Augustus into his stall, removed the saddle, and got a brush to rub him down.

"I got up and you were gone," Randall told him.

"You were tired, and I wanted to go for a ride. Clive was here earlier to see to the horses, but I told him I'd take care of Augustus when I returned."

"But…," Randall started.

"Look, I needed some time so I could think, and I always do that better when I'm riding." He paused his brushing. "I know what you want, and I'm grateful for the offer. I really am."

"But you're telling me no?" Randall said.

"No. I'm saying that I need a little time to get my head around it. Staying here is a lot of change. It's not just being with you, but everything is going to be different. I have to figure out what my place here is going to be and if that is going to make me happy." He continued with what he was doing. "I know you care for me, and I feel the same way. I think we can be happy. But you know that love isn't enough. We each have to have our place. You were born into yours, and whether you like it or not, you are the earl and have everything that goes with it. The people here all respect you and think a lot of you. Maybe more than you think of yourself."

"I'm sure that isn't true."

"But it is. Your people come to me with their issues because they don't want to bother you with them. It's like you're too important for them to bother you. I don't get that, but maybe it's just something inherent in the society here."

"But you do have a place. You'd be my partner. Everyone already comes to you with their problems because you're approachable, at least to them."

"I don't want that," Sawyer said. "I don't want to be thought of as an extension of you."

Randall sighed and stepped into the stall. "You aren't. Think of it this way. Society in this country goes back hundreds of years. We're all born into it, and our role in society, especially in a small village, is ingrained in us. People defer to me because they have always deferred to the earl. I carry a lot of weight simply because I own so much of the area. And they feel that if they get on my bad side, they could be evicted.

I know that some of my predecessors did that, and these people have a lot to lose. I would never do that to anyone, but they don't know that."

"I get that."

"But you're more approachable, and they like you. You're accessible, and everyone feels they can talk to you." Randall slipped his arms around his waist. "Why do you think I opened up to you?" He kissed the back of Sawyer's neck, sending a zing down him. "Everything about you says that you are easy to be with and that you know how to keep a secret. You aren't going to blab whatever you hear around the village. So if you want my advice, go with it. If you want a role, then I think this is it. You'd manage the repairs and upgrades to all the estate buildings. I trust you to do it well, and the people already know that you'll do your best for them."

Sawyer huffed. "Fine. If that's what you want me to do, then how can I argue with it? But I'm serious. There's a lot of work to be done, and it's going to take money, so we're going to need to figure out additional sources of revenue."

"I'm still not sure about the 'tea with an earl' thing. It's too close to playing on my title. And I don't want to do that. But there are some other ideas that I have. Maybe we can sit down with Celeste and the other estate staff and get some of their input."

"Fine." He slowly turned in Randall's arms and kissed him softly. "I need to finish up, and then I have a window to fix. Maybe you can set up this meeting with the staff, because we are going to need funds sooner rather than later."

"Okay. I'm on it." Randall left him alone with the horse, and Sawyer finished the brushing before leaving the stall to get to work.

"ALAN," SAWYER said into his phone as he paced along the verge that stretched out through the main lawn. "I need your help." If anyone could help him cut through the hamster wheels in his head, it was Alan.

"What's wrong?" Alan asked.

"Nothing, or I don't know if anything is wrong. Randall has asked me to stay." He swallowed hard.

"That's great." Alan sounded happy. "But you aren't sure you want to."

"I wish it was that easy."

"Okay. I'll tell you that it was hard for me to leave home and come here. I'm not going to lie to you. Some people accepted me, while others didn't. But there will always be folks like that, and I say screw them. You can't live your life on what others think."

"I get that. But how did you fit in? We're cowboys, and George and Randall live in a world that seems almost unreal. When does the other shoe drop?"

"Let me ask you this. Does Randall love you for who you are? Has he ever expected or asked you to change?"

"No." Sawyer wouldn't anyway. "He likes me for who I am."

Alan was quiet. "The real question is how you feel about him. Randall can't leave. His role is too tied to the estate and the people on it. He may be able to leave for a few weeks or a month, but he can't just chuck it all and move to Wyoming to be with you. It isn't going to work that way. So know that. It is the way it is. The question you have to answer is, do you love him enough to stay and make a place for the two of you? Make that pile he lives in a home? A *real* home?"

Sawyer swallowed. "What about all the legal stuff?"

"Leave that to Randall. Cutting through red tape is something earls and dukes are very good at. Besides, if the two of you get married, then some of the issue resolves itself. But don't let that put you off."

Sawyer paused. "I guess I need to figure a few things out."

"You do. But there's one more thing. There are a ton of men in this world, but you kiss a lot of frogs before you find a prince—or an earl or a duke, for that matter. When you find one, don't let him get away."

"Did you have a productive day?" Randall asked as Sawyer came in through the personal entrance after wandering the garden for a while after his call with Alan.

He sat in one of the overstuffed chairs and put his feet up. "Let me tell you. I fixed the sill for Charles and worked on the roof for his neighbor. All I could do was a temporary repair that will last a year at the most." He pulled out his phone. "I'm sending you a note that the roof at number 12 will need to be replaced." Sawyer sent the message. "I've done plenty of roofing, so I was thinking that maybe we could determine which four or five need to be fixed first and ask the community to chip in.

I know how to do roofing, and as long as they aren't thatched, we should be able to get the work done." He closed his eyes.

"Good. And I think I've identified the four cottages that need upgraded electrical and plumbing first." Randall turned away from his desk. "And I'm working to try to come up with how to pay for all of this."

"And…?" Sawyer said.

"I can't add more regular tours. But what do you think about a secret passages tour? We could add one or two a day. No more than that. They would need to reserve them in advance. And on that tour, we could include the servants' back stairs and maybe a look into some of the other servant areas. They would need some sprucing up, but much of it's on the third floor. The basement work areas aren't in any condition to be opened. What do you think?"

"If Celeste can handle it, then I'd try it out and see if you get any interest." He cleared his throat.

"I know what you're going to say. You're like a dog with a bone with this tea thing." He rolled his eyes. Sawyer knew he was wearing him down.

"Well, I love the idea, and I'd pay to have tea with you… as long as you served coffee." God, he wanted to good strong cup of coffee. Hell, he'd kill for one about now. "But I guess I have something I have to know. Are you sure about me staying here with you? Is that what you really want?"

Randall stood and strode over to where Sawyer sat and plopped down onto his lap. That was new, and damn, Sawyer liked it—a lot. "Does this feel like I'm serious?" He leaned against Sawyer's chest. "In case you have any doubts, then yes. I want you to stay here, and I want to see where things go between us. I've spent way to many years looking for something—or someone—and now that I found you, I'm not going to let you go."

"I see." Damn, it was heady being wanted so badly. Sawyer smiled, dropping his hat on the floor next to the chair. "Then as long as you're serious and you know what you're in for, I'll stay. But there are some conditions."

"There are?"

"Yes. We need some dogs. This place really needs some dogs running around."

Randall smiled. "I like dogs."

"Great. That that will be easy. We have to have more horses, and if you put me in charge as the estate steward, then you let me do the job and don't stick your nose in all the time. And lastly, you agree to try out my tea idea."

Randall growled. "Fine. We'll try it out, but if I have to do it, then so do you."

"I love it when you make that sound."

Randall pressed his lips to Sawyer's ear. "And I really love it when you fuck me while you're wearing your hat."

Now it was Sawyer's turn to growl. Randall slipped off him, and Sawyer took his hand and led him up the stairs. He paused outside of Randall's room, realizing it was their bedroom now. He liked that idea and tugged Randall inside before kicking the door closed. Sawyer opened the buttons on his shirt and shrugged it off. Then he kicked off his boots, watching Randall shiver. "Does all this talk mean that you love me?" Sawyer suddenly needed to know, and he wasn't going to beat around the damned bush. He stalked closer, watching as Randall nodded. "I need the words; I need to hear it."

Randall stepped back against the bed as Sawyer tugged at his shirt. "Yes. Of course I love you. I have since before we left Wyoming, but I didn't dare let myself believe it. What if you didn't come with me? What if you did and then went home? I had to make sure it was real."

"Well, it is." He pulled off his jeans and got Randall naked, which meant yanking off his shoes and shucking the man of his pants. "I love you, Randall." He leaned over him, pressing him onto the mattress. "I sure didn't love your attitude at first. But you won me over when you showed me the real you." He manhandled Randall as he climbed on the bed. "And you stole my heart." He didn't dare look away from Randall. Not that he could if he tried. The man was sexy as hell, especially heaving for breath with his eyes as wide as saucers. Sawyer fumbled around until he found the supplies and then got Randall ready before slowing sinking into the man. He was way too keyed up to take it slow. Tonight, after the entire estate was in bed, he'd make love to him for hours, but right now, at this minute, he needed to claim Randall as his.

Randall groaned as Sawyer sank deeper, his breathing fast. Sawyer closed the gap between them, kissing him hard as he drove the final way, filling Randall, joining them physically as well as by their hearts.

"You're mine and you always will be. Know that. I love forever, and I'm damned selfish when it comes to those I love," Sawyer said between kisses, not giving Randall much of a chance to say anything. Not that words were really needed. Randall's body told him everything he needed to know, from the sheen of sweat on his chest to the way his mouth hung open as Sawyer pulled away and slowly pushed into his tight heat.

"Fuck, that was some declaration." Randall wound his arms around Sawyer's neck. "It's a good thing I don't share well with others either." He groaned as Sawyer picked up the pace, rocking the bed. "I love you too." Randall arched his back. "And fuck, you're sexy in that hat."

"You like making love to a cowboy?" Sawyer asked, seating himself deep inside Randall.

"I think I always will." Randall groaned as the heat and excitement between them grew to a fever pitch. Sawyer didn't dare close his eyes. He wanted to remember this moment, the way Randall's eyes sparkled and then darkened as their passion continued to grow. Sawyer let loose all his desire, his mind floating as he drove them up a mountain of ecstasy. His control stayed with him right up to the point where Randall cried out, his entire body shaking under Sawyer as he tumbled into his release. The sight of him in the throes of passion was more than he could take, and Sawyer plummeted into his own climax, holding Randall with everything he had.

"Damn," Sawyer whispered a while later. His hat had tumbled off at some point and now rested cockeyed on the floor. Not that he cared. Sawyer held Randall in his arms, his eyes closed, fatigue and afterglow covering him in a blanket of sheer contentment. "I'm sure I have things I should be doing, but I can't remember what they are."

"I know just how you feel," Randall said as he reached for his phone. "I don't know about yours, but my calendar is empty for the rest of the day."

"Thank goodness." Sawyer snuggled closer before yawning and closed his eyes once more. "I do have a question, though."

"About what?"

"Well, if we get married, what does that make me? If you married a woman, then she would be a countess."

Randall chuckled. "You're suddenly very up on your British titles. I didn't think you cared about that sort of thing."

"I don't. Not really. But it seems to a lot of people here that titles and addressing people properly is a big thing. Everyone calls you your Lordship."

"Yes, they do. It goes with the title. George gets called your Grace. That's the proper address for a duke, and a duke's wife is addressed as duchess or her Grace as well, depending on the situation. It's all very confusing a lot of the time."

"I'm just going to call him George." All this was enough to make his head spin. "I guess I want to know if people are going to start calling me your Lordship. Because that's not what I want. I just want to be me, Sawyer Kincaid."

"I hate to say this, but there will be people who might do that, especially after we're married. That is if you want to get married." Suddenly Randall seemed unsure of himself.

"Let's talk about that down the road. There's no need to rush. But I don't want anyone calling me your Lordship."

"Fine. Then what should they call you?" Randall rested his head on Sawyer's shoulder. "There isn't another title for earl, and no provision was made for same-sex couples."

"That's great. I'll just be me and that's the end of it."

Randall lay still for a minute and then lifted his head, those incredible eyes filled with mischief. "I've got the perfect title. You can be the earl's wrangler. I admit, it's a bit of a mouthful—"

Sawyer tightened his hold on Randall. "Maybe, but that I can live with." And he intended to do just that for a very long time.

Epilogue

RANDALL PULLED his coat tighter around him to keep out the winter chill as he and Sawyer walked up the drive from their morning ride. The last six months had been pretty amazing for both of them. Randall had eventually broken down and agreed to a trial run of Sawyer's afternoon tea idea. He had limited it to twenty people besides himself and Sawyer. The spaces had sold out in less than an hour, and in the end, Randall had enjoyed it much more than he thought he would, so they were working on a schedule for the next season.

Sawyer took his hand as they walked the garden paths toward the house, pulling Randall out of his thoughts. "What are you stewing about?"

"The tea thing," Randall admitted.

Sawyer snorted. "Again?" That mischievous grin was back. "You need to let it go and admit I had a great idea. Mrs. Cook is going to run the entire thing, and it's only once a week. She loves the idea, and all you need to do is show up and be the handsome, amazing man I fell in love with."

Randall couldn't argue with Sawyer, not when he looked at him like he hung the moon.

"What's this?" Sawyer asked as they approached the house. A black BMW sedan was parked off to the side of the drive. Sawyer stayed with Randall as the car door opened and a man climbed out.

"Arthur," Sawyer said happily and checked the time. "Did I forget about an appointment?"

He shook his head. "I'm sorry to drop in unannounced, but I was in the country and received some news, so I headed right out here." They shook hands.

"Come inside," Randall said, ushering them all into the great hall and then through the maze of sheet-covered furniture to their living quarters. "I know it seems kind of forlorn, but everything would be caked with dust otherwise."

Their rooms were warm, and Randall offered Arthur a seat. Poppy, the Yorkshire terrier they had rescued from a shelter, jumped up and settled next to Sawyer. He sat on the other side of the man he loved with everything he had, girding himself for whatever news Arthur had to deliver. "I didn't want to speak about this over the phone."

"All right."

"As you know, your father had filed a petition against your uncle's estate, and that held things up in probate, but all that has been cleared now." He bit his lower lip.

Sawyer nodded. "I understand that. Do you know where my father is?" Sawyer asked, slowly petting Poppy.

"Yes. He's somewhere in Florida at the moment, probably still dodging debt collectors." Arthur smiled. "One of the people he owes money to actually filed a claim against any proceeds he might get with the probate court. That convinced them that your father was still gambling, so the estate has been cleared and the assets have been released to you. I will make arrangements for the money to be transferred to your account. I have a list of his other assets. You can look them over and decide what you wish to do with them."

"Thank you," Sawyer said somberly. "I wish I'd had a chance to know him. That's what I really would have wanted."

Arthur pulled out a case from his bag and handed it to Sawyer. "Your uncle requested that this be given to you. It was found among the papers he kept with our firm. There was one for your father as well, but in accordance with your uncle's wishes, that disk has been destroyed."

"So my father is actually still alive," Sawyer said.

"Yes, but we know little more than that. Has he contacted you again?" Arthur asked.

"Not in months," Sawyer answered. "Is it wrong to say that I'm relieved?"

"No," Randall said softly. "He's caused you enough hurt." Both their fathers had, and it was time for the two of them to live good, happy lives and move past their issues with fathers who should never have been parents.

"I'll leave the two of you to get on with your day. I just wanted to bring you the latest news." Arthur stood, and Randall did the same before seeing him out to his car. When he returned, Sawyer had the DVD in the player.

"Huh?" Sawyer huffed.

Randall sat next to him once again. "Is that your uncle?" Randall asked.

"Yeah, I guess. I think maybe I do remember him a little from when I was a child." He unpaused the message.

"You don't need to watch this now," Randall said.

"It's okay." He pressed Play and the message began.

"Sawyer, I know I didn't have much of a chance to get to know you. Your father made sure that was pretty much impossible. But I did keep an eye on you as best I could." The images changed to a picture show.

"That's me singing in school when I was about ten," Sawyer said before the image changed. "My high school graduation." Sawyer swallowed hard, and Randall took his hand and held it firmly.

"I wish things had been different, but I was there for some of your life, even if your father didn't know it. I know that things didn't turn out the way I would have liked, but I hope you'll remember me in some way. Use the money and the things I left behind to better your life, and above all, be happy." The message ended, and Sawyer sat still, other than lightly stroking the dog.

"I am happy," Sawyer said before taking a deep breath. "Okay. That part of my life is over, and it's time to just let it all go."

"Do you think you can?" Randall asked.

Sawyer shrugged. "Maybe we both can… together." Then Sawyer pulled him into a hug, and they held each other for a long time.

THE FOLLOWING morning, Randall shivered and wished he'd stayed in bed. Part of him loved this time of the year. The estate was closed for the season, so there were no tourists around and the landscape was quiet, with just the wind and the occasional whiff of woodsmoke on the air. But the cold—he hated the cold and the fact that it was nine in the morning and it seemed like the sun had had a hard time getting up as well.

When he'd risen, there had been a note next to the bed asking him to get dressed and come out the main doors. Sawyer had said that he had a surprise for him and Poppy. Randall had to admit that he was more than a little curious.

Then he heard it, a sound that carried on the wind: bells. He looked around, at first to make sure he was hearing correctly, but they grew louder, and then an open carriage pulled by two horses came into view. For a second, it seemed like he had been transported back to another age.

"You're doing well." Sawyer's voice carried on the wind as the horses drew close enough that Randall could see Clive was driving. Once the carriage pulled up in front, he came to a stop, and Sawyer climbed out.

"What is all this?" Randall asked.

Sawyer climbed down. "This is your surprise." He held the door so Randall could get in. Poppy settled right on the seat, looking out, tail wagging like this was his chariot. "After I managed to get those roofs fixed, Mr. Waverly in the village approached me and took me to his garage. Off to the side, he had this, and he asked if I wanted it as a thank-you. I insisted that I pay for it, and we agreed on a price. Clive helped me, and we fixed it up. I've been teaching him how to drive it."

Randall settled in the seat. "Where did you get the horses?" These certainly weren't Caesar and Augustus.

"I borrowed them for the day… sort of on approval." Sawyer told Clive they were ready, and the carriage started forward. Clive didn't turn around and sat straight on the seat. "I want to buy them and use them as draft horses. Having the carriages and buggies is nice, but we should be able to use them." He spread a blanket out over their legs and settled back, both of them nestled in the comfortable seat, Poppy tucked in right beside them.

"You really want to do this?"

Sawyer turned to him. "I have a plan. We're going to need six horses, but we can start with these two. And we can offer buggy tours through the estate grounds. They would be half an hour at most, and we could offer up to four a day. We already have the paths we could use. Can you imagine it?" They turned off the main drive onto one of the paths through the grounds. Suddenly it was like they were gliding into the past, the world slowing down—at least for a while.

"I'll have to think about it," Randall said softly as Sawyer slipped an arm around him, tugging him close. The cold receded, and it was just the two of them. Randall sighed, turning his head toward Sawyer, who kissed him gently, but with just enough passion to banish the cold and make him glad for the blanket covering his lap.

Sawyer chuckled. "Thanks."

"I haven't said yes," Randall said.

Sawyer nuzzled his neck. "Yeah, but you didn't say no, and I have plenty of ways to get you to agree. If my figures are correct, it will bring in enough money to pay for two renovations a year, once we're truly up and running, so to speak." He slipped a hand under Randall's shirt. Randall smiled and soaked in Sawyer's heat. "Look," Sawyer said as they crested the rise on the south lawn. Randall turned, taking in most of the estate in a single view. "That's a view I never get tired of."

Randall looked into Sawyer's eyes. "Me too." He leaned against Sawyer as Clive started the horses forward once more until Clive pulled the carriage to a stop again. Sawyer fidgeted under the blanket.

"I wasn't sure what the proper thing was to do for this, so I figured I'd go traditional." He slipped from under the blanket and knelt on the floor of the carriage.

"Sawyer," Randall said softly, this throat aching.

"Will you marry me?" Sawyer asked, opening a ring box. Poppy woofed softly as though urging him to agree.

"Yes… of course I will." Sawyer slipped the ring onto his finger, and Randall pulled him into a kiss. "You beat me to it."

"Huh?" Sawyer said.

"I have a ring for you up in my dresser. I was going to ask you this weekend." Randall chuckled as Sawyer sat back down. "When do you want to do this?"

"I was thinking next spring."

"Sounds perfect." Randall pulled the blanket up around them and settled back, holding Poppy and leaning against Sawyer as the carriage rocked them lightly back toward what he'd finally come to feel was truly home.

Keep reading for an excerpt from
Eastern Cowboy
by Andrew Grey

BRIGHTON LOST track of the amount of time he sat in his grandfather's rocking chair. It was warm enough, and the breeze felt perfect. But after a while the sounds and activity intruded. He stood up and used his cane to steady himself as he walked to the edge of the porch. Off to the west, a huge condominium complex stretched as far as the eye could see: light blue aluminum-sided buildings with white trim that seemed to go on forever. On the other side, a shopping center rose at the edge of his grandfather's land—now his land. And he knew that behind the house was a subdivision of one- and two-family homes crammed together on postage stamps of land. Sure, he knew he could get a lot of money for the land, possibly millions, but this was an oasis of green in a forest of tacky modern homes.

"You're up," Brianne said.

"Just thinking," Brighton said without turning around.

"The house is decent and very well built, that's for sure, but it needs to be updated. Badly. The kitchen is the one Grandma used, and nothing has been changed. There are things you're going to need to do and fast. The electrical service is old and will need to be replaced, and there isn't any air-conditioning. I went down into the basement, and it's clean as a whistle, but I saw the electric box. I think Thomas Edison invented it along with his lightbulb."

"How do you know stuff like that?" Brighton sure as hell didn't.

"I read a lot, and I'm a science geek. I love stuff like electricity, magnetics, and how things work. You should know that."

"I guess." Brighton laughed. "I remember when Mom and Dad got you a battery-operated Barbie car. You played with it for a few years and then took it apart to see how it worked." Brighton turned around. "Do you think it's safe to live in?"

"Of course. You just need to call an electrician and have some work done. Everything is doable, and you're going to want air-conditioning. How Grandpa lived without it is beyond me, but you're going to have to have it, especially since window units might start blowing fuses. There's a whole box of them in the basement."

Brighton nodded. "Let's look around." He turned and went inside. The place looked just as he expected and remembered. The living room had the same sofa and chairs it had always had. It was like stepping into a time capsule locked away for fifty years.

"I checked the upstairs, and there's going to need to be a lot of cleaning. Everything is covered in dust. It doesn't seem like it's in bad condition or anything, just neglected."

"Well, it isn't going to get less neglected with only me here." Stairs were a problem for Brighton. Especially full flights—he hated the things. But then again, maybe it was time for him to figure out how to navigate them and move forward.

"There are some big bedrooms and a huge bath. Clean things up, and you'll love it." Brianne grinned. "The bathroom is heaven. It's old, but dang, the room is really big. There's space for an army. I'm almost jealous. I remembered it being big as a kid, but sometimes memories get distorted."

He wandered through the main floor, then stopped at the foot of the stairs and peered upward. "I wonder if there are still animals. They'll need to be fed and watered if there are. Lord knows our aunt and uncle would let them starve in their rush to sell." He turned away from the imposing stairs. He could figure that out later.

"I'll go check. But I'm not cleaning any stalls. I didn't dress this morning for farm work."

Brighton hadn't either. Hell, he'd figured he might get a small inheritance and that was it. "I'll go with you. Together we can probably keep anything from starving to death." He hoped. Brighton walked slowly, closing the front door behind them. Brianne strode across the yard to the small barn and pulled open the door. Brighton stepped inside. Animals bleated and baaed. A pony lifted its head, staring at him with doleful eyes. He peered over the stall wall and saw an empty manger and water trough. "Fuck," Brighton swore and looked around. He found a bale of hay and managed to get the twine undone and drop some hay in the manger. "Is there a bucket?"

"I found one back here. Nothing has water, and most all the mangers are empty," Brianne called back as she pulled open a door. "There's feed in here. Thank God it's labeled. I don't know how much to give, but we can do our best."

"I'll handle the feed if you'll get the water. Start with the pony."

Brianne agreed and began hauling buckets of water from the tap just inside the barn. Neither of them could find a hose, so Brighton added that to his growing mental list of things to get. He also added another item to the "things that scare the shit out of me" list as well as the "how the fuck am I supposed to do this on my own" list. How his grandfather had watered the animals was beyond him, but he always was stubborn, and things had to be done his way.

One-handed, he got feed to the four goats and four sheep. Brianne made sure they all had water. "We might as well let them out into their pens if we're going to be here a while." She opened doors, and after a while the animals wandered outside into their enclosures. Then she joined Brighton in the center of the barn. "I can come over for a few days to help with cleaning and make sure the animals are fed. But this place needs more help than I can give."

"I know," Brighton sighed. "I keep thinking I should just sell and give everyone their money. I hate to do it, but I can't take care of a place like this. I manage to take care of myself, and that's about it." This was overwhelming in the extreme.

"Breathe, big brother, and take it one step at a time. There aren't so many animals that it's a huge job. There are nine total." She rolled her eyes. "There aren't herds of goats and flocks of sheep. Get on the Internet, find out how to care for them, get a hose, buy feed, and go at it. It will be good for you to care for something other than just yourself."

Brighton could feel his chest pounding and gasped for air. He closed his eyes and pushed away the panic that started to rise. "It's too much."

"It is not!" she told him firmly. "Now get over it, and stop feeling sorry for yourself. You were given a gift today, so don't squander it." She placed her hands on her hips and glared at him. "Where is the man who stood up to Aunt Vera when we were kids and told her to go to hell when she said she didn't think I should go to college? As I remember, you told her that I was going to college because 'I was going to make more of myself than a stupid cow like her.'" Brianne grinned. "You had spunk and confidence."

"That went away a long time ago."

"Well, get it back, because the mousy Brighton is starting to get on my nerves." In that moment she sounded just like their mother. "Rather than concentrating on what you think you can't do, figure out what you can. The rest you can find people to help you with." Brianne stepped out of the barn and into the sunshine. "This is a small piece of heaven in the midst of suburban sprawl. Or it could be. This could be your piece of heaven. You don't have to do what Grandpa might have done or listen to anyone else. Make it yours."

"How in the hell did you get to be so smart? I'm the big brother. It's my job to give you advice."

Brianne scoffed and smiled at him. "Please. I was always the smart one, and you know it." She put her arm around his shoulder. "Now let's go in the house and see what's good for now and what needs to be done." Brighton nodded and followed Brianne back into the house. "I'm going downstairs to get a bucket I saw." She left, and Brighton heard her on the stairs. She returned with buckets that she'd filled with every cleaner she seemed to be able to find. Then she hauled dusters, brooms, and the cleaning gear upstairs.

Brighton pulled out his phone and the card from the lawyer. He called the number and asked to speak to Mr. Granger. After a few seconds, his call was answered. "Mr. Granger, I think I'm going to need some help."

"Please call me Arthur, and I'll do what I can."

Brighton explained about the visit from his aunt and uncle.

Arthur was none too pleased. "We'll use that to our advantage if they start causing trouble."

"Good. Brianne and I are at the farm, and it's evident that I won't be able do this on my own. The animals didn't have food or water when we got here."

"I was told by your aunt that they would take care of them."

"Well, I doubt they did that. There was nothing left at all. Anyway, we got the animals sorted, and they're going to be fine. If your cousin would be interested, he's welcome to stop by the farm tomorrow afternoon, and we'll talk."

"Very good. But I want to stress you aren't under any obligation. If you don't want to hire him, I'll understand."

"I appreciate that. Thank you. We'll talk and then see what we both think." That was all Brighton could promise, but he was a little desperate.

"Fair enough." Arthur paused, and Brighton heard papers rattling. "Your aunt called a while ago. Apparently she's still interested in making the funeral arrangements. Your grandfather has been cremated already, and his wish was to have his ashes scattered at the farm."

"Brianne and I will do that after the service."

"She said she had to move the memorial service to Sunday."

Brighton swore under his breath. "It needs to be on Saturday. Sunday Brianne is receiving her degree, and she isn't going to miss that. Aunt Vera is being mean." Brighton took a deep breath. "I'm assuming from what you said that you are acting as executor."

"Yes."

"Good. Then go ahead and lay down the law with her. We already had the pleasure of doing that today. I guess it's your turn." Brighton smiled.

"I didn't want to cause any undue family strife."

"Too late for that," Brighton quipped.

"I'll handle everything from this end."

"Thank you." This was ridiculous, and he wasn't going to put up with Aunt Vera being a pain. How could she do this to her own father? Let him rest in peace, and let the family say good-bye. "I appreciate all the help. I just can't deal with my aunt's pettiness right now. I could sic Brianne on her, but we might end up with a double funeral and then a murder trial."

Arthur chuckled. "I'll handle it."

"Thank you," Brighton said. He hated putting him in the middle of a family fight, but his aunt was being vindictive, and he didn't have the energy to fight with her right now.

"Were you on the phone?" Brianne called down from upstairs.

"Yes. The attorney is going to send his cousin over tomorrow. Don't know if he can help or will be interested, but I have to try." Brighton paused while he decided what to tell her. "Vera is up to her tricks. She said that she needed to move the memorial service to Sunday."

"That witch!"

"Don't worry. I sicced the attorney on her. He'll take care of it. She had already made arrangements and things, so the old bat is just being mean."

Brighton's leg began to shake, so he went back outside and sat in the chair on the porch. He should go upstairs and try to help Brianne, but the ache in his leg said he'd done what he could do for today. "I hate this," he said out loud. The truth was, he felt useless most of the time. He could work and was good at what he did, but functioning in the real world was a pain in the ass. He couldn't drive. He didn't have enough muscle control in his right leg to depress the accelerator and brake pedal with any degree of finesse. For three months he'd kept hoping his leg would improve. The doctors said it would, but it hadn't happened yet.

His phone rang, and Brighton answered it even though he didn't recognize the number.

"Hello, is this Brighton?" a man asked in a very measured way.

"Yes."

"I'm…. Tanner. Is it… okay to come by… tomorrow at… nine?"

After confirming with Brianne that she could drive him to the farm in the morning, Brighton said, "Of course. I'll meet you here at the farm. Do you have the address?"

"Yes." He expected the man to repeat it to him, but he didn't.

"All right. I'll see you then." Brighton wondered what was up. Arthur had said his cousin didn't talk much. Suddenly he didn't have the greatest feeling about this.

Brighton sat for a few minutes until guilt over doing nothing while Brianne worked got the better of him. He leaned on his cane and opened the door. His grandfather thought he could do this or he wouldn't have left him the farm, and Brianne thought he could as well, so he needed to gird himself and just do it.

Brighton walked to the base of the stairs and looked upward. He took the first step. "Bree," he called. She appeared at the top of the stairs. "Come take my cane." She hurried down the stairs and took the cane from his hand. Then he put both hands on the banister and made his way up the steps.

"Why are you doing this?" Brianne asked when he was halfway up.

"Because I need to get around my own damn house if I'm going to live here." He didn't mean to snap, but it came out that way. Brighton was sweating by the time he made it to the top. He took his cane when Brianne offered it. "So, what are we doing?"

They spent some time cleaning a few of the rooms of dust and cobwebs. He mostly stripped beds and cleaned out drawers of linens that had seen better days. Brianne good-naturedly went up and down the stairs for him. "I think I need something to eat, and we've done enough," Brighton declared, stifling a cough. The dust was becoming too much for both of them. They had found some fans and had placed them in various windows to blow the air out of the house, and that helped.

"At least I got a room cleaned that you can use if you like." She gathered the supplies and placed them in the bathroom. "I'm filthy and need a shower." Brianne took Brighton's cane and his arm and helped him down the stairs, which was much easier than going up. "I just have one question: After I shower and change, where are you taking me for dinner?"

They reached the first floor without incident. "Wherever you'd like." Brighton took his cane and started for the front door. "But before I feed you, we need to make sure the animals are fed and inside before we leave for the night."

"Slave driver," Brianne quipped and hurried out to the barn. He heard her inside, calling and swearing, but she eventually returned. "They're in. None of them wanted to come until they heard the food. Everything is closed up, but I'm afraid the pens will need to be cleaned soon. And I draw the line at poop shoveling."

Brighton rolled his eyes. "I used to change you when you were a baby."

"Don't go there," Brianne warned. "You used that for years, but it isn't going to work anymore and neither is the story about the time I wet you. Guilt all you want—I'm not cleaning pens. Did you lock the house?"

"I will." He turned and closed the door then used the key the lawyer had given him to lock the door. "I think I should have the locks changed. I probably should have had that done today." He chewed on his lower lip. "I'll see to it tomorrow."

"If anything's missing we'll call the police and tell them what happened. They'll search Vera and Raymond's house so fast. They'd be stupid to try again." She paused, shaking her head. "Do you want to stay?"

"No. I want to go home." It had been a hell of a day, and Brighton needed a chance to think. "Come on. You can clean up at my place, and I'll order delivery. We can relax, and you can tell me about what you're interested in studying." Most of the time he had no idea what the hell she was talking about when it came to her work, but he always listened.

"Nope. I want to watch mindless television and think about nothing."

"Amen." That was the best idea he'd heard all day.

Brianne ended up spending the night on his sofa. They stayed up late and were falling asleep already, so he wasn't about to let her drive home that late. In the morning, after working the kinks out of his leg, Brighton dressed and made breakfast. It wasn't much, just bacon and eggs, but the scent had Brianne sniffing around the kitchen before her eyes were fully open. "God…."

"Sit, eat. Then we'll go."

"What time is it?" Brianne looked around for the clock.

"Eight. Tanner is coming to the farm at nine." Brighton put eggs on each plate along with some bacon. Then he added extra slices to Brianne's plate and handed it to her. Brighton knew the way to her heart: pork. She ate, still half-asleep, leaning over the table.

"I can't believe you got me up at the ass crack of dawn." Brianne wasn't a morning person.

"Please. It's eight, and I fed you." Brighton chewed on a slice of bacon.

"You're forgiven."

"Good, because we need to go in ten minutes." Brighton backed out of the line of fire and finished eating. Then he carried his dishes to the sink and waited for Brianne to finish. He put her dishes in the sink as well, and she humphed away, returning a few minutes later dressed but looking like hell.

"You're on your own today. I have things I have to do, but I'll come back to the farm before dinner and bring you home. I suggest you make sure you have something to eat."

"I'll order delivery," he quipped. They left his apartment, and she drove him to the farm. Brighton thanked her and got an unintelligible response from her. "At least help with the animals before you leave."

She turned off the engine and unfastened her seat belt, muttering the entire time. She didn't stop as she went to the barn or let up as she was opening doors and shooing the "beasts" outside. "They have water and feed. The rest is up to you. I'll see you later."

Brighton met her at the barn door and saw her stop, eyes widening. "What is it?" he asked as he followed her stare. "Oh…," Brighton added as one of the biggest men he'd ever seen walked down the drive in a cowboy hat, tight jeans hugging tree-trunk thighs, and a flannel shirt that look about ready to bust at the seams if the man breathed too deep. "Jesus," he whispered, watching as the man got closer. Brianne, who had been in an all-fired hurry to get away, suddenly stood stock-still. Not that Brighton could blame her. He blinked twice and stepped out of the barn, taking slow steps as he leaned on his cane. The man got close enough for Brighton to see blond hair poking out from under his hat and eyes as blue as the summer sky.

"Hello," the man said in a deep resonant voice. "I'm T-Tanner."

Brighton leaned on his cane, breathing hard, his mouth dry. Damn, the man was gorgeous in a rugged, had-a-hard-life kind of way. He pushed those thoughts aside, though, because they weren't appropriate on so many levels. First thing, this guy could snap him like a twig if he wanted, and second, hell, if he hired this man, then he wasn't doing anything with an employee. *Stop*, he silently yelled at himself. He was getting way ahead of things.

"I'm Brighton, and it appears I've inherited this place, but as you can probably guess, farm chores aren't something I can really do." Brighton began moving toward the house. "How did you get here?"

Tanner pointed toward a motorcycle parked out near the road. Brighton wondered why he'd parked it way out there but didn't ask. And Tanner didn't seem too keen on talking.

"I'm Brianne, his sister." Brianne reached to shake Tanner's hand. Tanner looked uncomfortable but shook her hand.

"Didn't you have things to do?" Brighton asked Brianne. She smacked him on the shoulder.

"I'll see you later," Brianne said, laughing as she walked to her car. Brighton waved as she got in and then drove away. Then he turned back to Tanner. "Can we go talk on the porch? I need to sit down. My leg hurts because I've been standing too long." He hobbled across the yard and climbed the two steps, then sat down in the rocking chair. There were days when he felt so damned old. Brighton motioned to the other chair, and Tanner perched on the edge of it like he was ready to run away at any second. "Arthur told me that you worked on a ranch in Montana."

Tanner nodded and reached up to lift his hat off his head. He placed it in his lap and nodded again. Brighton got no further answer.

"What kind of work did you do?"

"Ranch… stuff."

Brighton waited but didn't get any further elaboration. "Did you make repairs?"

Tanner nodded.

"Take care of horses and animals?"

Tanner nodded again without speaking, but his attention was clearly on Brighton.

"I need someone to feed and clean up in the barn and help with repairs around here. My grandfather hadn't been able to do a lot of things, and it's hard for me to haul and carry." It was hard for him to know he was getting his point across. Arthur had said his cousin didn't talk much, but he hadn't said he was nearly mute. "Do you understand?"

Tanner opened his mouth, but no sound came out at first. "Yes. I can… help." Tanner stood up, and without any further word, he walked over toward the barn and disappeared inside. Brighton sat a minute and was about to get up to see what was happening when he saw Tanner hauling a wheelbarrow full of mucked bedding out of the barn. He looked around and must have seen the muck pile. Tanner emptied it and returned to the barn without a word.

Brighton wasn't quite sure what had happened, but it seemed he'd hired himself some help. He'd have to explain to Tanner what he needed, but from the looks of things Tanner knew what he was doing and was willing to get his hands dirty. Brighton could do some things on his own, but many were beyond his capabilities. One thing he needed to do was to get Internet and his work equipment set up in the house if he was going to be spending his days here. For the first time since speaking with the lawyer, he felt that things just might work out. But then again, things had a habit of going to hell just when he thought he was out of the woods.

ANDREW GREY is the author of more than two hundred works of Contemporary Gay Romantic fiction, including an Amazon Editors Best Romance of 2023. After twenty-seven years in corporate America, he has now settled down in Central Pennsylvania with his husband of more than twenty-five years, Dominic, and his laptop. An interesting ménage. Andrew grew up in western Michigan with a father who loved to tell stories and a mother who loved to read them. Since then he has lived throughout the country and traveled throughout the world. He is a recipient of the RWA Centennial Award, has a master's degree from the University of Wisconsin–Milwaukee, and now writes full-time. Andrew's hobbies include collecting antiques, gardening, and leaving his dirty dishes anywhere but in the sink (particularly when writing). He considers himself blessed with an accepting family, fantastic friends, and the world's most supportive and loving partner. Andrew currently lives in beautiful, historic Carlisle, Pennsylvania.

Email: andrewgrey@comcast.net
Website: www.andrewgreybooks.com

How can they be together when
they live in different worlds?

The Duke's Cowboy

ANDREW GREY

Cowboy Nobility: Book One

George Lester, the Duke of Northumberland, flees familial expectations in Britain for the promise of freedom of San Francisco, looking for the chance to be himself. But before he even gets close, a blizzard forces him off the road, and he finds himself freezing half to death in a small town with no motel… with a litter of puppies to look after.

Luckily for George, he also finds Alan.

As the heir to his family's ranch, Alan Justice knows the burden of being the oldest son. He doesn't have time to show George, the stranger his brother dragged home, what it takes to be a cowboy. But that very night, George surprises him by helping a mare in distress through a difficult birth. Maybe the duke is made of sterner stuff than Alan thought.

George and Alan keep surprising each other, and every day they grow a little closer. But when George's responsibilities call him home, Alan finds he's the one who has something to prove—that he can handle what it means to be the duke's cowboy.

Scan the QR code below to order

The Viscount's Rancher

COWBOY NOBILITY ♥ BOOK TWO

ANDREW GREY

Cowboy Nobility: Book Two

Viscount Collin Northington has spent his life under his father's thumb. When his friend George and his cowboy husband, Alan, offer to let him tag along to the US for two weeks, Collin jumps at the chance to get away. Perhaps the open ranges of Wyoming will put his problems into perspective. He even dreams of meeting a cowboy of his own.

He doesn't expect his dreams to come true.

When Tank Rogers returned home after his military service, he took over the family ranch the way he knew he was meant to. Now he's the only one left, but he likes the solitude. Even so, he has no excuse to object to putting up Alan's friend for a few weeks in exchange for some help around the ranch—it wouldn't be neighborly.

The feelings he has for his blue-blooded houseguest aren't exactly neighborly either.

Once Tank realizes there's more to Collin than upper-crust manners, suddenly his solitary life holds a lot less appeal. But in the long term, Tank doesn't fit into Collin's fancy society life any more than Collin fits into Tank's down-home and dusty ranch... does he?

Scan the QR code below to order

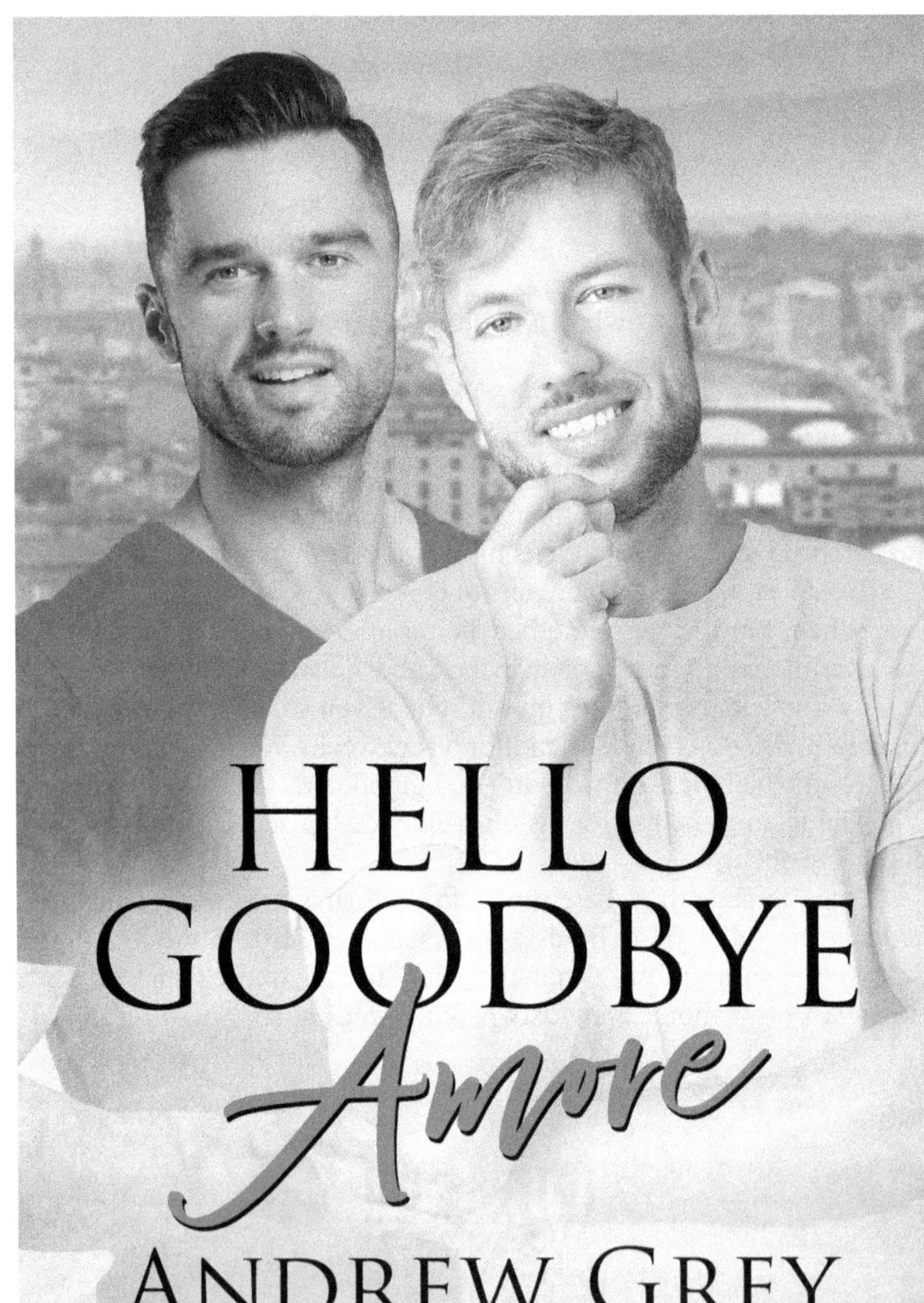

HELLO GOODBYE
Amore
ANDREW GREY

In college, Chase Anderson and his twin sister, Elaine, met Antonello Glorioso and became best friends. Chase fell in love with him—but so did Elaine, so he kept quiet. Then heartbreak happened: they graduated, Antonello returned to Italy, and Elaine died, leaving Chase to raise her son as his own.

Returning to Florence to run the family business had felt like Antonello's only option. He did his duty to his legacy, but he's been second-guessing that decision since he got on the plane. Still, he doesn't know what he could've had until it shows up on his doorstep.

Chase never wants to see Antonello again. His departure tanked the business the three of them had planned to start and hurt his sister deeply. But his engineering project needs specialized metals, and the Glorioso firm is the best supplier. Reluctantly, Chase agrees to head to Italy for a few months to oversee production, hoping he'll be able to keep a low profile… only to run into Antonello the first day.

As Chase and Antonello spend time together, old hurts fade, replaced by renewed friendship and the possibility for a love they've only fantasized about. But duty, family, history, and big secrets could topple any possibility of a future.

Scan the QR code below to order

HUNKS OF THE MONTH

ANDREW GREY

Former fashion photographer Sterling Vaughn reached the pinnacle of his profession only to have his life and heart come crashing down around him. Now he's attempting to rebuild his life as a portrait photographer in the town where he grew up.

Connor Hillyard is proud of his Scottish ancestry and dresses accordingly. The civic-minded college history professor has spent more of his life collecting degrees than experience. His only family is his sometimes matchmaking great-aunt Lucille, who thinks nothing of pulling him into her community gardening projects.

When Lucille needs a photographer for a calendar project to save her failing garden club, she recruits Sterling, who ropes Connor in as a model. Their eye-opening hunky gay calendar pulls the two men closer together. But just as things get interesting between them, the calendar polarizes the town, threatening to pull Sterling back into the high-profile world of fashion and away from the man who brought his heart back to life.

Scan the QR code below to order